CASE FILE 13

EVIL TWINS

To our border collie, Pepper.
There was never a more faithful
or friendly dog. I hope there
are lots of juicy bones for
you in heaven.

Case File 13 #3: Evil Twins
Text copyright © 2014 by J. Scott Savage
Illustrations copyright © 2014 by Douglas Holgate
All rights reserved. Printed in the United States of America.
No part of this book may be used or reproduced in any manner whatsoever without written permission except in the case of brief quotations embodied in critical
articles and reviews. For information address HarperCollins Children's Books, a
division of HarperCollins Publishers, 10 East 53rd Street, New York, NY 10022.
www.harpercollinschildrens.com

Library of Congress Cataloging-in-Publication Data
Savage, J. Scott (Jeffrey Scott), 1963-
    Evil twins / J. Scott Savage.
        pages   cm. — (Case file 13 ; #3)
    Summary: "Nick, Carter, and Angelo bring their monster expertise on a
camping trip to the woods, where they accidentally unleash creatures that have
the power to copy human appearance exactly"— Provided by publisher.
    ISBN 978-0-06-213337-3 (hardcover bdg.)
    [1. Best friends—Fiction.   2. Friendship—Fiction.   3. Imaginary creatures—
Fiction.   4. Shapeshifting—Fiction.   5. Monsters—Fiction.   6. Camping—
Fiction.]   I. Title.
PZ7.S25897Evi   2014   2013032820
[Fic]—dc23   CIP
                                                                    AC

Typography by Sarah Nichole Kaufman
14 15 16 17 18   CG/RRDH   10 9 8 7 6 5 4 3 2 1
❖
First Edition

CASE FILE 13

EVIL TWINS

J. SCOTT SAVAGE

HARPER
An Imprint of HarperCollinsPublishers

Questions in the Night

Come in. It's late, but I've been waiting for you. How did I know you'd come back? Your kind always does. Oh, you might tell yourself that the last adventure was too dreadful, too horrifying. You might convince yourself that you're done delving into mysteries that can only be solved after dark. But eventually you are drawn by an irresistible hunger—a hunger for the unknown. A hunger that can only be satisfied by what we both seek.

I notice you keep looking at my mirror. Is it just me or does it almost appear as though the figure behind the glass is not your reflection at all, but a darker version of yourself, watching you with terrible eyes?

But never mind. I'm sure you're tired of listening to an old man babbling about his fears. Doubtless you're dying to know what is happening to the three boys whose adventures I've been carefully documenting in Case File 13.

It seems they are off on a camping trip. One to the forest, and no ordinary forest at that. The woods are dark places—some even older than I—full of legends, mysteries, and creatures never seen by the eyes of men.

At least, no men who lived to tell the tale . . .

CHAPTER 1

SETTING SAIL . . . OR SHOULD IT BE DRIVE?

Saturday morning was the perfect day for a campout. The sky was blue and, although it was early December, the temperature was nearly sixty-five degrees. Nick and his friends Carter and Angelo had been looking forward to this trip ever since Nick's dad announced it. But now Nick was afraid the trip was going to end before it even got started. Mom was digging through the gear in the back of the car like a cat hunting a mouse, while Dad complained from the driveway behind her.

"Did you bring the sleeping bags?" Mom asked, pushing aside a stack of air mattresses.

"Of course," Dad said, hands on his hips.

"First-aid box?"

"Complete with snakebite kit, instant ice packs, and suture set."

Mom looked through a grocery bag, set it aside, and examined every canteen individually.

"Is she always like this?" Carter whispered.

Nick stepped away from the SUV so his parents couldn't overhear him. "Dad's got kind of a reputation for forgetting things when we go camping."

Angelo pushed his new glasses up on his nose and peered toward the car. "What *kinds* of things?"

"Well, once he brought a whole bunch of fancy dehydrated food but nothing to cook it in."

"How bad could that be?" Carter asked, dumping a pack of cherry Pop Rocks into his mouth.

Nick made a face. "Ever tried sucking on a mouthful of dried shrimp Rangoon, waiting for it to get soft enough that you could chew it? Trust me, it's not pretty. Another time he packed the tent but forgot the spikes. In the middle of the night, this freak storm picked up the tent and rolled us all down the side of a hill into a lake."

Angelo's eyes widened in alarm. "Maybe I'll go help your mom check on things."

Carter stuck out his tongue to make the candy in his mouth pop louder. Red-colored saliva splashed from

his mouth with each pop.

"Dude, stop spitting," Nick said. "That's disgusting. And what's with the hair?" Carter was always changing his hair color. One month it was neon green, the next it was blue. But this was the first time he'd ever dyed it black with white down the middle.

"Zebra stripes," Carter said, swallowing the Pop Rocks. "Tell me it's not the coolest yet."

"*It's not the coolest yet,*" Nick repeated. "I hate to tell you, dude, but you look like a skunk."

"That's cool too," Carter said, opening another bag of Pop Rocks. "Are we still planning on making s'mores?"

"Yeah," Nick said. "We're making s'mores. I made sure Dad packed the marshmallows, graham crackers, and chocolate." Sometimes he wondered if Carter was able to stop thinking about food for more than a minute or two at a time.

"Well?" Dad asked, holding his hands palms up as Mom climbed from the back of the car. "Are you ready to apologize and admit I didn't forget anything this time?"

Mom brushed her hands on the front of her jeans. "I'm not apologizing until we actually set up camp. But I can't see anything you missed."

"Never doubt genius," Dad said, closing the hatch. "Let's go, everybody. It's time to set sail on the adventure of a lifetime."

"I think we've had *more* than enough adventures to last a lifetime," Mom muttered under her breath. "I'd settle for a nice, normal campout."

"*Normal?*" Dad grinned, clearly elated by his victory. "Were Lewis and Clark satisfied with normal? Did Cortés want a simple campout? Was Magellan scared of a little adventure?"

Angelo scratched the back of his head. "Actually, Magellan was killed by natives."

Dad scowled. "Get in the car."

"How come I have to sit in the middle?" Carter complained as the three boys slid onto the back bench seat.

"You're the shortest," Angelo said.

Carter snorted. "Short people get no respect."

Nick's dad started the car and pulled out of the driveway as Mom programmed the GPS.

"Where's the campground?" Angelo asked.

"Near Santa Cruz." Mom craned her neck to look back at the boys. "I'm so excited to see the tide pools."

"The tide pools are fascinating," Angelo said. "And the monarch butterflies should be there for their winter migration."

Angelo never failed to surprise Nick with his knowledge. Of course he knew everything there was to know about monsters, monster movies, alien abductions, and anything else paranormal. It was what had drawn the Three Monsterteers, as they called themselves, together in the first place. But he seemed to know about everything else, too.

"*Butterflies*?" Carter scoffed. "I'm planning on catching a mermaid. I brought a couple of Almond Joys. Mermaids go crazy for coconut."

Nick's mom rolled her eyes and turned to face the front.

"Where did you hear that?" Angelo asked.

Carter shifted in his seat and pulled a small booklet out of his back pocket. "Right here." He opened the book, which was called *Finding and Catching the Lovelies of the Sea*. "Mermaids are vegetarians by nature," he read, "living primarily off of seaweed and algae. However, they have been known to crawl onto shore for a rare treat of fresh coconut."

Angelo opened his monster notebook and started writing, but Nick shook his head. "What would you do with a mermaid if you caught one?"

"Drop out of school and take her on the road," Carter said at once, as though he'd been giving it a lot

5

of thought. "Do you have any idea what people would pay to see a live mermaid? I'd probably have to teach her to do stuff. You know, like card tricks, or juggling flaming chain saws."

"I dated a mermaid once," Dad said as he pulled onto the freeway. "Things went swimmingly at first. Then her scales starting rubbing me the wrong way and—" Mom cut him off with a stare, and he quickly changed the subject. "Wait till you boys see my new camp stove. It's a beauty. Three burners, adjustable windscreen. It even has a built-in cook timer."

Angelo nodded, clearly impressed. "What kind of fuel does it take?"

"*Fuel?*" Dad's face went white as he looked toward the back of the car.

"Tell me you didn't forget fuel for the stove," Mom said.

Dad braked, hung his head, and got off at the next exit.

CHAPTER 2

THIS IS WHY YOU SHOULDN'T READ—OR GORGE YOURSELF—ON CURVY ROADS

"Here's the thing I don't get," Nick said as his dad steered up the winding Highway 17 through the Santa Cruz Mountains. They'd been driving for just over an hour and were less than thirty minutes from the beach. "If a vampire bit a mummy, would the mummy turn into a vampire, stay a mummy, or form some weird combination?"

"Definitely stay a mummy," Angelo answered without even stopping to think about it. "Mummies don't have any blood for the vampire to infect."

"Sure. I get that. But does it have to infect the blood? I mean, couldn't the vampire just inject his venom into the mummy's flesh and turn its mummy cells into vampire cells?"

Angelo shook his head. "Assuming we're talking about a sanguivore—the kind of vampire that feeds off blood, not energy—vampires suck in blood from the victim, mix it with their venom, and kind of spit it back out. The blood is how the venom mixes into the rest of the victim's body. Sort of like what Carter does with food. Except he never spits out anything he eats."

Carter gave him a dirty look. "I'm right here, you know."

Nick considered Angelo's words for a minute, staring out the window at the dense forest passing by outside. "Then if a mummy and a vampire got into a fight, I would totally bet on the mummy. They have supernatural strength and excellent endurance. Plus, they are immune to pain and have all kinds of cool curses."

"Not all mummies have curses," Angelo said, flipping through his monster notebook. "And even if they do, the curses might not work on vampires. More importantly, vampires can fly, and they are much smarter than mummies."

Nick smirked. "How can you possibly know that?"

"Simple." Angelo pointed to a picture of a long hook in his notebook. "Mummies don't have any brains. When the embalmers prepare the body, they shove this

through his nose and—"

"That's disgusting," Mom said, spinning around to glare at the boys from the front seat of the car. "Can't you think of something fun to do until we get to the campsite? When I was a girl we used to sing songs while we drove."

Dad grinned back at them in the rearview mirror. "'Ninety-Nine Bottles of Beer on the Wall' was one of my favorites."

Nick wrinkled his nose. "So you'd rather have us sing a repetitive verse about an alcoholic beverage we won't even be able to legally drink for ten more years ninety-nine times?"

"No!" Mom exploded, giving Dad the evil eye. "Why don't you play a game? You can look for the letters of the alphabet on license plates."

"No offense," Nick said, "but I think I'd rather watch my fingernails grow."

Mom frowned. "All right. How about I Spy?"

"That could be fun," Angelo said. He looked out the window for a minute. "I spy something with sharp fangs and snakes for hair."

"A gorgon," Nick said. "That was easy." He looked out his window. "I spy something with four legs and the head and wings of an eagle."

9

"Trick question. If all four legs are lion legs, it's an opinicus. But if the front legs are aquiline, like an eagle's, it's a griffin. Of course if the back legs are . . ."

Mom turned away with a sigh, muttering something that sounded like "Why couldn't I have given birth to a girl?"

Carter, who had been going through snacks as if he hadn't eaten in a week, looked up from the mermaid book he'd been reading and wiped his forehead. "Are we going to be on this curvy road for long?"

"Do you feel sick?" Mom asked.

"A little," Carter said. His stomach gurgled so loudly it sounded like a milk shake in a blender.

Nick studied his friend's face. "You do look sort of pale."

"Look straight ahead," Dad said. "You don't want to throw up. Once, when I was a kid, my dad drove us up this majorly curvy road. That made my stomach feel sort of queasy. But then he fed us these smelly meat chunks that turned out to be eel jerky, and—"

Carter's face turned from white to green. "Pull over," he said, clutching his hands to his mouth.

Nick's father pulled the car off the highway, and before Nick could even get his seat belt off, Carter was scrambling over him and clawing for the door handle.

"Eel jerky? *Really*?" Mom groaned, shaking her head. "You tell a sick boy about the time your sadistic father fed you *eel jerky*?"

Dad held out his hands. "He didn't let me get to the end of my story. It turned out that even though the eel jerky smelled terrible it made my stomach feel much better. Or was that the Pepto-Bismol my mom gave me? Come to think of it, the eel might have . . ." He glanced out the window to where Carter was gagging on the side of the road. "Maybe you better go help Carter. I think he just threw up an armchair."

"You. Are. Impossible," Mom said before getting out of the car.

Dad looked back at Nick and Angelo. "There was another song we used to sing about a kid who eats a bad peanut and dies. But that might not be the best song either."

A few minutes later, Carter climbed into his seat, sipping from a bottle of water Nick's mom had given him.

Mom got back into the car, slamming her door so hard it rattled the drink in her cup holder. She looked at the boys. "Until we get to the campground, no food, no reading, and no disgusting stories. Clear?"

"Yes," the boys answered together.

11

"Roll down both of your windows a little so Carter can get some fresh air. And you," she said, looking at Dad. "Drive slower, stop suggesting inappropriate songs, and no more stories of any kind."

Dad opened his mouth as if he was going to argue, but then he thought better of it and restarted the car.

"Feeling better?" Nick asked as they pulled onto the freeway.

"I guess," Carter said. "Man, it felt like my gut was trying to turn inside out." He wiped his mouth with the back of his hand. "Actually I feel pretty good now."

"Not surprising." Angelo glanced up at Nick's mom before whispering, "Getting sick to your stomach feels gross because your body is telling you not to do whatever made you sick in the first place. Throwing up releases endorphins that make you feel better so the vomiting doesn't seem as bad."

Nick groaned. "Who knows stuff like that? What do you do, study books about puking?"

"I study books about everything," Angelo said in a tone of voice that made it clear he couldn't understand why everyone didn't do the same. "You never know when something will come in handy. Say an alien abducts you and makes you eat poison. Knowing when to puke and when not to could make all the difference."

Mom started to turn around and the boys quieted down.

"Speaking of aliens," Carter whispered. "When I was, you know, yakking, something weird happened."

"Please don't tell me your puke formed the shape of a flying saucer," Nick said. A couple of years before, Carter had gotten on a kick where everything formed some kind of symbol. Clouds looked like werewolves, trees looked like dragons. Nick and Angelo finally put a stop to it when he wanted to describe the shapes of things that really shouldn't be discussed.

"No," Carter said. "Although now that you mention it . . ."

Angelo held up a finger. "Don't go there."

"Fine," Carter said. "Besides, that's not what I wanted to tell you."

"What *did* you want to tell us?" Angelo asked, twirling one hand impatiently.

Carter waved Nick and Angelo closer. "Okay. When I was throwing up—which actually looked more like a pepperoni pizza than a flying saucer—I think something was watching me from just inside the woods."

"An animal?" Nick asked, hoping it was a raccoon and not a bear. True, they were going to be camping near the beach. But if there were bears in the woods,

13

and they smelled something tasty like beef stew—or a kid—they might come exploring.

"I don't think so. I heard a branch crack when I first got out of the car. But I wasn't paying much attention because I was . . ."

"We know what you were doing," Angelo said. "Get on with the story."

Carter started to take a bag of M&M's out of his pocket, but Nick put a hand over the bag. "Better not."

"Yeah." Carter reluctantly put the bag back. "Anyway, I heard this branch crack and I thought I saw something in the shadows. When I looked in its direction, it disappeared into the trees."

"It probably *was* an animal," Angelo said. "When Nick's dad pulled the car over, it came to see what was going on. Then, when you got out, you scared it. There are lots of animals in these woods. Squirrels, raccoons, deer, mountain lions. Even bears."

Nick bit the inside of his cheek. *So there* are *bears. Great.*

"It wasn't an animal," Carter said, his eyes wide.

"How could you tell?" Nick asked. "Did you see it?"

Carter shook his head. "I didn't see it. I *heard* it."

Angelo ran his fingers across the pages of his notebook, his eyes intense. "What did you hear?"

14

"I heard it . . ." Carter swallowed and his hand went to the bag of candy in his pocket. "I heard it say something."

Nick felt the back of his neck grow cold. "You mean like words?"

"Uh-huh. I heard it say . . ." Carter lowered his voice so that Nick and Angelo had to lean close to make out what he whispered. "I heard it say my name."

CHAPTER 3

NEXT TIME, USE A TRAVEL AGENT
TRAVEL AGENT

Nick couldn't help snickering a little. "A bear called your name?"

Carter glowered. "I didn't say it was a bear."

"Did it say Scooby-Dooby-Doo?"

"Actually Scooby-Doo was a dog," Angelo said. "Yogi was a bear. He did talk, but he said things like 'Is that a picnic basket?' and 'I'm smarter than the average bear.'"

Carter ground his teeth together. "It wasn't a bear or a dog. And it didn't say anything except my name."

Realizing Carter was upset, Nick tried to stop smiling, but it wasn't easy. "Maybe it was some kind of sugar rush."

"You guys make all the food jokes you want. But I'm telling you, someone—in the woods—said my name. I heard it as clearly as I'm hearing you now. It sounded kind of like a kid."

Angelo pulled a ballpoint pen from his notebook and chewed on the end. "Technically, it's possible there could have been someone hiding in the woods. And they could have overheard one of us say your name. But why would they repeat it? Especially if they were hiding?"

If Carter had an answer, they didn't get to hear it, because at that moment Dad called out, "Here we are!"

Nick looked out the window at a big wooden sign with the words SANTA CRUZ BEACH STATE CAMPGROUND stenciled on the front. A bulletin board below the sign was covered in papers that read things like "Don't feed the animals," "No open campfires," and "No loud music after 11:00 p.m."

"Look," Mom said, pointing to a grove of eucalyptus trees. Thousands of monarch butterflies fluttered about, filling the air with clouds of black and orange. Even Nick, who didn't care much about insects of any kind, was impressed.

"Sure are a lot of old people," Carter said, craning his neck to look out the window.

Nick's gaze shifted from the butterflies to the nearest campsites as his father pulled the car behind a long line of motor homes making their way to the entrance. Carter was right. There were nearly as many old folks as there were butterflies. Old men in baseball caps and flip-flops. Old women in bathing suits and wraparound skirts. Nick couldn't see anyone who looked younger than seventy.

"The last time I saw this much white hair was at a polar bear convention," Nick's dad said with a chuckle.

Mom looked worried. "Maybe it's some kind of event." She turned to Dad. "You *did* make a reservation, didn't you?"

Dad acted offended. "Of course I did." He pulled a piece of paper from his shirt pocket. "Got it right here."

As the line of motor homes crept slowly toward a small booth where a man in a ranger's hat was checking papers and giving directions, Carter whispered, "I bet the local grocery store is completely sold out of prune juice and denture cream."

"That's a total stereotype," Angelo said. "Some of those guys look pretty tough. I'll bet at least half of those men could beat you in arm wrestling."

"And at least that many of the women," Nick added.

"Who said anything about arm wrestling?" Carter

asked. "I'm just hoping they all go inside their motor homes at seven thirty and sleep so we can go mermaid hunting. My book says the best time to catch them is just after sunset."

As the vehicle in front of them pulled through the entrance, Nick's father drove up to the ranger's booth. "Name?" asked a tired-looking man holding a clipboard.

"Braithwaite," Dad said cheerfully. "Looks like you've got quite a crowd here."

"Senior butterfly watchers," the man said, looking down at his paperwork. "They come from all across the country this time of year to see the monarchs."

Mom smiled. "We're pretty excited about them ourselves."

The man with the clipboard frowned, his tanned forehead wrinkling. "What did you say your name was again?"

"Braithwaite," Nick's dad said. "B-R-A-I-T."

The man flipped up the paper on his board, checked the one under it, and shook his head. "Sorry. I don't see you anywhere on the list."

Mom's smile began to fade. But Dad held out his paper. "I've got the reservation right here. I made it months ago."

Nick's stomach began to tighten. "Please don't let this be another one of Dad's screwups," he whispered to himself.

The ranger took the sheet of paper and looked it over. "There's the problem," he said, nodding.

Nick began to feel better. It was probably just some kind of computer error.

The ranger held out the reservation and turned it so Nick's dad could see it. "This is for February, not December."

"What? Let me see that." Dad grabbed the paper, read over it, and looked at Mom, who was biting her lower lip.

"Huh," Dad said, rubbing his chin with one hand and turning back to the ranger. "I don't understand this. I'm sure I put December in the computer."

Nick's heart sank.

"Any chance you could squeeze us in?" Dad smiled weakly.

"Maybe a week from now," the ranger said, glancing back at the long line of vehicles waiting to get into the campground. "But this week I couldn't get my own grandmother in, even if she offered me a hundred dollars to do it."

Nick looked from his dad to his mom, expecting her

to blow up. Instead she only looked sad.

"Wish I could help," the ranger said. "Maybe you can check the other campgrounds. Or possibly a hotel."

"Sure," Dad said, turning the car around so he could drive back out. "They can't *all* be full."

But they were all full. Every campground, hotel, and motel they tried within twenty miles said the exact same thing. "Senior butterfly watchers have everything booked up solid." The longer they looked, the sadder Nick's mom seemed, and the more determined his dad grew to find an opening.

By the time they checked the last hotel in town— a hole in the wall that looked like only the dirt on the paint was keeping it from collapsing into a pile of splintery boards—the sun was beginning to set.

"I think we better go home," Mom said. "Everyone's hungry and tired."

Dad sighed and pulled back onto the freeway. "I feel terrible."

"It's not your fault," Mom said. "Mistakes happen."

"Sure," Nick chimed in. "We can come another time. Who wants to stay in a crowded campground anyway?"

Angelo stared silently out the window as they drove up the twisty highway.

21

Nick leaned over and quietly asked, "Are you bummed out because we didn't get to see more of the butterflies?"

"What?" Angelo jerked his gaze from the woods. "Oh. No, I'm sure we can see them another time."

"Why so quiet then?" Carter asked.

Angelo tapped his fingers on the car window and looked at Carter. "I've been thinking about what you heard out there."

"The kid?"

"What if it wasn't a kid?" Angelo asked. "What if it wasn't even human?"

Nick narrowed his eyes. "What are you saying?"

Angelo opened his monster notebook to a page with a series of names written in bold red ink. Momo, Yowie, Meh-Teh, Raksha, Kikomba, the Great Bear, Yeti, Sasquatch.

"Bigfoot?" Nick asked, unsure if Angelo was joking.

Angelo flipped the page to where a picture of a large, hairy creature was pasted next to a map of the Santa Cruz Mountains. The map was covered with blue dots, each of which had a date written beside it.

"June 1980," he said. "Two campers smelled something like rotting garbage. A few minutes later, they heard snapping branches and a twelve-foot-tall creature

came running down the side of a hill."

He tapped another dot. "In 1998, a family thought they saw a really big homeless guy dressed in animal fur."

"Maybe it *was* a homeless guy," Carter said. "You know, one of those hermits."

Angelo pointed to a picture of a deep, animal-like footprint. "Not unless he had feet six inches longer than a size-twelve shoe." He flipped through several pages of notes. "There are dozens of reports of Bigfoot sightings in this area."

"Where did you get all this stuff?" Nick asked. He knew Angelo collected a lot of monster information. But this was amazingly detailed, even for him.

Angelo opened his pack and took out the new iPad his mom had given him for a birthday present the week before. He tapped a few links and pulled up a website with a picture of a large, hairy creature next to a map of the United States. "The Bigfoot Field Researchers Organization. I've been following them for years. But I looked a little more closely when I knew we'd be near here."

Carter stared out the window at the darkening woods. "So somewhere in those trees there might be a twelve-foot-tall beast with feet the size of snowshoes?"

At that moment, the car jerked to the right and Nick's head banged against the window. "What happened?" he yelped as his dad pulled the car off the freeway. He stared out the front windshield, halfway sure they'd just hit a Yeti.

"Didn't you see the sign?" Dad cried. "There's a campground here with openings."

CHAPTER 4

THE SWEET SMELL OF PINE TREES, CAMPFIRES, AND PREPACKAGED, ARTIFICIALLY FLAVORED SNACK FOODS

"I'm not so sure about this," Mom said as Dad steered the car slowly down a narrow road.

"What's not to be sure of?" Dad asked, staring into the darkness ahead of them. "You wanted to go camping, and that's just what we're doing."

"I wanted to go camping in a state campground near the beach. This looks like the kind of area where you'd hide a dead body."

Nick had been looking forward to this trip for weeks. But although he hated to admit it, he sort of agreed with his mother. The road they were on didn't look like anyone had driven over it in years. Weeds poked up through the middle of the asphalt and the trees seemed to be getting closer and closer to the road the farther they went. "Are you sure there's an actual campground here?" he asked.

From where he was sitting, Nick saw his dad's jaw clench. "Maybe I forgot the stove fuel. And maybe I made the reservation for the wrong month. But I *can* read. I definitely saw a sign that said SWEET WATER CAMPGROUND. NO RESERVATIONS REQUIRED."

"I think it's awesome," Carter added. "The woods look totally creepy. I'll bet we run into a Sasquatch before we even get unpacked."

Mom turned around, her lips pressed tightly together. But Dad laughed it off. "Sure we will. And a dragon too. And brownies riding unicorns."

"You brought brownies?" Carter asked, rubbing his stomach.

Angelo elbowed him. "He's talking about the little people, not the snack. And, from what I've read, most of them live in Scotland. So the idea of seeing one of them here—especially riding a unicorn—is rather preposterous."

"Not any more preposterous than running into a large, hairy creature that doesn't exist," Dad said.

Angelo shook his head and clucked his tongue

against the roof of his mouth, but didn't say anything more.

"Look!" Dad hooted as he drove the car off the road into a small gravel lot. "We made it!" He pulled forward and the car's headlights illuminated a dirt clearing with a rock fire pit and a few logs dragged up beside it.

Nick leaned over the seat to get a closer look. "This is it?"

Dad pulled the car a little farther in and bumped against a wooden sign. He waved his hands at the tall redwoods surrounding them. "It's magnificent. Look at those trees. They've got to be five hundred years old at least."

Mom frowned. "There are no picnic tables. No bathrooms. I don't even see a water spigot. What kind of campground is this?"

"The best kind." Dad opened his door and drew in a deep breath. "Smell that fresh air? No crowds. No RVs. No blasting stereos. Makes you wonder why we even considered being packed in like sardines with those ancient butterfly watchers."

Nick stepped out of the car and looked around. The air *did* smell good—sort of like Christmas trees. And it definitely wasn't crowded. In fact, as far as he could

27

tell they were the only ones there. "Are you sure this place is open?" he asked, staring into the darkness. Beyond the car, there wasn't another light anywhere. What kind of campground had no lights, no tables, and no people?

"Dude, this is sweet!" Carter said, bounding out of the car. "Let's go see if we can find Bigfoot tracks."

"Hold on now," Dad said. "You don't want to go running off in a place like this. These woods go for miles. You could get lost."

"Or eaten," Angelo said under his breath.

"Shouldn't there be a ranger or something?" Mom asked as she stretched her legs. "Where do you check in and pay your fees?"

"I imagine a ranger will come around at some point." Dad grabbed a flashlight out of the car and pointed it at the weathered sign that was now tilted into a pine tree from where he'd bumped it with the car.

Nick walked up beside his dad and stared at the words painted on the dark wood. *Gefahr! Bleiben Sie weg! Kein Campingplatz! Wandern, angeln und jagen verboten!*

"I think it's German," Angelo said.

"What does it say?" Carter asked. "If it mentions

anything about sausages and sauerkraut, I'm there."

"Don't ask me," Mom said. "I took four years of French."

Dad scratched the back of his neck. "I took a year of German in high school. But mostly so I could sit by Hannah Holmes. What a cutie she was. The only thing I memorized was '*Möchten Sie ins Kino gehen Samstagabend?*' 'Would you like to go to the movies Saturday night?' Unfortunately every time I asked her, she said *nicht.*"

Mom glared at him.

"Let me try translating it," Angelo said. He typed the phrase into his iPad before shaking his head. "Darn. No service."

"Look," Carter said, pointing to one of the words. "*Campingplatz.* Could that mean camping?"

"Sure," Dad said. "I think that's right. Maybe I got more out of that German class than I thought. I'm pretty sure it says, 'Welcome. Plenty of spaces. This is the best camping. Set up a tent, relax, and have dinner.'"

Mom's mouth twitched. "Either that or 'Your husband is an idiot and you're all going to get killed in your sleep.'"

29

"Well, if we're going to die, let's do it on a full stomach," Dad said. "Who's going to help me set up the camp stove?"

Carter raced after him. "Anything that will get the food here faster. I could eat an entire pizza all by myself."

Nick chuckled as Carter continued to name every food he could think of. "I don't think he's completely clear on the concept of camping food." When Dad did the planning, most everything they ate was add-water-and-mix. And the last time Nick checked, there was no such thing as dehydrated pizza.

Angelo continued to study the sign under the illumination of the moonlight.

"Any idea what it really says?" Nick asked.

"No," Angelo answered. "But that's an awful lot of exclamation points for a welcome message."

Nick sighed, hoping this wasn't going to be another trip where something disastrous happened.

Fortunately, things went more smoothly than he could have imagined. Dad got the stove going with no problem and even managed to light a fire. Mom took over the cooking while Dad and the boys set up a pair of tents, inflated the air mattresses, and dug a latrine

30

behind a nearby tree. Dinner—chili, corn on the cob, and biscuits—was delicious. They even made s'mores for dessert while Dad told a story about a one-eyed miner who discovered his mine was actually home to a giant demon.

"Who knew your dad was such a good storyteller?" Carter asked, licking marshmallow off his fingers.

"I think camping brings it out in him," Nick said. He looked up at the stars that filled the black velvet sky and had to admit things had worked out pretty well.

Yawning, Mom got up and began putting away the food.

"Wait," Carter said, reaching for the marshmallows. "I wasn't done."

"Any more sugar and you'll be up all night," Mom said.

"She's right," Angelo agreed. "Remember that time you were sleeping over at my house and ate an entire bag of peanut butter cups right before you went to bed? You got up in the middle of the night, sleepwalked out the front door, and started shooting baskets at three o'clock in the morning."

Carter sulked. "I told you. It had nothing to do with the candy. I was dreaming I had to beat Godzilla in

a game of HORSE or he was going to destroy New Jersey."

"There are worse states he could pick," Dad said.

Mom just shook her head and rolled her eyes. "No more sweets and no more scary stories. I'm exhausted and the last thing I want to do is wake up in the middle of the night because one of you boys is having a nightmare." She walked around the fire and stopped in front of Carter. "Let's have it."

Carter looked up, his eyes wide and innocent. "What?"

Mom waggled a finger. "You think I don't know about your stash of sweets? Hand it over. I'll give it back in the morning."

Carter looked at Nick and Angelo as if checking to see which of them had snitched.

"You might as well give in," Nick said. "Moms have X-ray vision and a super sense of smell. She can tell if I've been wearing the same pair of socks for more than two days without even looking."

"Fine." Carter dug into his pants pocket and pulled out a bag of gummy worms.

"Keep going," Mom said, taking the candy.

Carter frowned and checked his other pockets.

One by one, a pair of Kit Kats, three Pixy Stix, a box of Junior Mints, and a package of mini doughnuts went from his pockets into Mom's hands. "That's it," he said, as he handed over the last item. "I hope you're happy. I'll probably starve tonight."

Mom pressed her lips together, weighing the pile of loot. "Unzip your jacket."

"What?" Carter's mouth dropped open. "That's everything."

"Give it up." Nick laughed. "I told you. X-ray vision."

Carter snorted and opened the front of his hoodie. Inside was a full package of Oreos.

"I'll keep an eye on those," Dad said, getting up from his log.

"Not a chance, buster," Mom said with a smirk. "I'm not having cookie crumbs in my tent attracting bugs and who knows what other creatures. I'm putting this all in the car, safely out of the reach of boys big and small." She turned to Nick and his friends. "Okay, time for bed. And don't stay up all night laughing and talking. We've got a busy day tomorrow."

As the boys took off their shoes and climbed into their tent, Angelo whispered, "Too bad about the cookies. Those would have been great to snack on tonight."

33

Carter peeked out the tent door to make sure Nick's mom wasn't watching and reached into his sleeping bag. A second later he pulled out a twelve-pack of Mountain Dew and another package of Oreos. He winked. "Double Stuf."

CHAPTER 5

I'VE OFTEN THOUGHT THAT TO A MONSTER, A TENT MUST LOOK LIKE A BURRITO

Nick was dreaming about being chased through his school by a mummy. Although the mummy should have been shuffling slowly along, in his dream it was racing up and down the halls on roller skates. A vampire rowing a boat past a bank of lockers told Nick to hide in the girls' bathroom. But even though the school was closed for the night, and there wouldn't be any girls in the bathroom, Nick was too embarrassed to go in. He was trying to convince the vampire to steal the mummy's skates when something jabbed him in the ribs.

"You can't make me go into the girls' bathroom," he mumbled.

"Who said anything about the girls' bathroom?" a voice asked.

Nick squinted into a blinding light. "What's going on?"

"Wake up," the voice said.

Nick realized someone was pointing a flashlight directly into his eyes. "Get that out of my face," he said, blocking the light with his hands. The flashlight moved away and in the darkness he could just make out Carter staring down at him.

For a moment Nick thought he was home in his room. Then he looked around and saw Angelo struggling to climb out of his sleeping bag.

"What time is it?" Nick asked, sitting up. As the sleeping bag slipped down to his waist, the cold air reached his arms and face, raising goose bumps.

"Almost three," Angelo said, after pushing on his glasses and checking his watch. "What are you doing waking us up in the middle of the night, Carter? If it's Godzilla again, tell him to find a new game."

Carter pointed his light toward the door of the tent. "I heard something out there."

"Are you kidding me?" Nick lay back on his air mattress and pulled his sleeping bag around his shoulders. "Go to sleep."

"No, really," Carter insisted. "I heard something outside, moving around."

Angelo ran his fingers through hair that poked up in every direction. "It's probably just a chipmunk or a squirrel."

"Trying to break into the car?"

At Carter's words, Nick pushed himself up. "Squirrels break into trashcans and coolers, not cars."

Carter gave an exasperated huff. "That's what I'm saying! Something is out there and it was trying to get into the car."

Angelo took off his glasses and polished the lenses on the front of his T-shirt before peering at Carter through the darkness. "Are you sure you weren't dreaming?"

"It wasn't a dream." Carter held the flashlight against his chest, his features oddly disturbing in the shadows created by the upward-facing beam. "I woke up a little while ago and had to go to the bathroom really bad. You know, because of all the . . ."

"We know. Because of the soda," Angelo said, twirling his finger to move the story along.

"Right. Anyway, it took me a while to find my flashlight, and once I did, I was getting ready to unzip the tent when I heard this shuffling sound—like footsteps."

Nick knew Carter would take an hour to tell a

37

five-minute story if you let him, and he could feel his eyelids beginning to droop. "Can you skip to the part about something breaking into the car?"

Carter grimaced. "I'd be there already if you two would quit interrupting me. So anyway, I was about to unzip the tent when I heard—"

At that moment, a metallic clicking sound came from outside the tent. Nick and Angelo turned toward the sound while Carter covered the lens of the flashlight with his fingers. "That's it," Carter hissed.

The three boys stared at the closed door of the tent as the sound came again—*click-clack, click-clack.* It could have been anything: a tin can banging against a rock, the camp stove rattling in the wind. But what it sounded like was the door handle of the car being raised and lowered.

"You think it could be your dad?" Angelo asked quietly.

Nick swallowed. "Maybe. But why would he be jiggling the door handle at three in the morning?"

They waited silently. Nick didn't know about the others, but he was getting seriously spooked.

The sound came again. *Click-clack, click-clack, click-clack.* Whoever or whatever it was seemed to be jiggling the handle over and over.

Angelo clutched his monster notebook to his chest like a shield. He looked at Carter. "Y-y-y-you've got the f-f-f-flashlight. Look and see what's out there."

"Are you kidding?" Carter asked, his eyes wide. "What if it's Bigfoot? I'd rather pee my pants." He rolled the flashlight across the tent floor to Nick.

"What kind of Monsterteers are you?" Nick whispered. But the truth was he didn't want to go outside either. It was one thing to talk about a twelve-foot-tall creature when you were sitting inside a warm, safe car. But here, in the middle of the pitch-black woods, with nothing between him and whatever was out there but a flimsy piece of nylon, the thought of an actual Sasquatch was terrifying.

He picked up the light with shaking hands, hoping that whatever it was would go away. Instead, the clicking was replaced by the sound of footsteps.

"It's coming toward us," Carter said, sliding to the back of the tent.

Something crackled just outside the door and Nick's throat closed to the size of a straw. "If that's you trying to scare us, Dad, it isn't funny."

The crackling stopped and the shuffling footsteps circled around the side of the tent. Whatever it was, it was just outside. Studying them? Waiting to rip the

tent open and eat them all?

The thought of being trapped inside the tent while some huge creature attacked was too much. With a gasp of fear, Nick yanked down the zipper and tumbled through the open door. Outside, the flashlight seemed completely ineffective against the overwhelming darkness of the woods.

"What do you see?" Angelo asked from inside the tent.

Swinging the beam left and right, Nick searched for a Sasquatch or a bear, or whatever had been outside. "Hang on," he croaked.

With trembling hands, and knees that felt like melted ice cream, he edged around the side of the tent. In his mind, he could just imagine glowing eyes staring down at him. Every branch seemed to be a reaching paw, every shadow a hulking figure. But although he was sure something was out there, he couldn't see anything more menacing than one of Carter's candy wrappers.

Slowly he began circling the tent.

"If it's Bigfoot, hoot like an owl," Carter called.

Nick gritted his teeth. "If it's Bigfoot I'm going to run for my life and let it eat you." By the time he had completely circled the tent—finding no creatures of any kind—his heart rate was beginning to return to

normal. He took a deep breath. "Whatever it was, it's gone."

Carter's head popped out of the tent door, swiveling left and right. "Are you sure?"

"No. I'm just trying to get you to come outside so it can eat you." Nick picked up the candy wrapper off the ground and handed it to Carter. "Don't litter."

Carter looked at the wrapper and frowned. "Hey, who ate my gummy worms?"

"What do you mean?" Angelo asked, crawling out the door next to him.

Carter held out the wrapper. "This is the wrapper from the gummy worms Nick's mom took from me. Somebody ate them."

"That's not the only thing someone ate," Angelo said, pointing toward the fire ring.

Nick turned to see an open Oreo package on the ground. He picked it up, making the same crackling sound they'd heard from inside the tent.

Carter climbed out of the tent and walked over, hugging his arms to his chest to keep warm. "If your dad ate all my snacks, he's totally buying me more."

Angelo came out of the tent, holding his own flashlight and shining it around the side of the tent. "Um, guys," he said, his voice sounding much higher-pitched

41

than normal. "I don't think it was Nick's dad that ate the cookies." He knelt on the ground, studying something in the dirt.

"What did you find?" Nick asked, coming over to join him.

"If it was a raccoon, I'm turning it into a coonskin cap," Carter said. "Nobody messes with my candy."

Nick was opening his mouth to tell Carter that he'd probably run screaming like a little girl if he ever came face-to-face with a raccoon, when he spotted what Angelo was looking at and the words froze in the back of his throat.

"Dude," Carter whispered. "Is that what I think it is?"

Nick collapsed to his knees beside Angelo and stared at a footprint in the dirt. It was smeared a little, as if whatever had made it was dragging its feet. But even in the dark of night, with the edges slightly blurred, it was clear that the print was at least twice as large as the biggest human foot.

CHAPTER 6

ALWAYS HAVE A GOOD BREAKFAST BEFORE GOING MONSTER HUNTING—JUST IN CASE IT'S YOUR LAST

Carter backed away, his face looking like someone had just shown him his own grave. "That's it. I'm out of here."

"Hold on a minute," Angelo said. "Let's think this through."

"Think what through?" Nick asked. He stared into the dark woods, waiting for the shadows to morph into a terrifyingly huge creature. All he wanted to do was wake up his parents, tell them what he'd seen, and get away before the Sasquatch came back.

"This is proof of Bigfoot." Angelo reached into his backpack and pulled out a small tape measure. He pulled the tape out and whistled softly. "Twenty-three inches."

43

"Are you out of your ever-loving gourd?" Carter asked. "You're actually taking measurements while a monster waits to eat us? Those Oreos aren't going to keep it full for long."

Nick had to agree.

Angelo snapped a couple of pictures with his iPad and wrote something in his monster notebook. "If it wanted to attack us, it would have done it already."

"That's what the kids always say in slasher movies before the bad guy cuts off their heads," Carter said. "Come on, Nick, let's wake up your parents."

Angelo put away his iPad and brushed pine needles off his hands. "What do you expect his parents to do?"

"Get us out of here," Nick said. "The faster the better." Every tree swaying or branch creaking was making him jump.

"That's assuming they believe us," Angelo said. "It's not like we've ever made up anything like this before. Right?"

Nick rubbed his mouth with the back of his hand. There *was* the time they spread chicken bones around the neighborhood to make it look like something was eating pets. And the time Carter swore he'd been attacked by a lightsaber-wielding alien to get out of a math test. And all three of them got suspended the time

44

they dug up the front lawn of the school, filled the hole with torn clothes, and left muddy footprints leading up to the front door. So he supposed there was a chance his parents might think they had faked this too.

"Even if they *do* believe you," Angelo said, "do you really want to leave here and give up the chance of a lifetime? The chance to track down a real live Sasquatch and get it on film?"

Nick couldn't believe what he was hearing. "You're saying you want to go after it?" They were all crazy about monsters. But this was bordering on complete lunacy.

Angelo patted his notebook against his leg. "Not tonight. It's probably long gone by now anyway. Let's clean up this mess so your parents don't suspect anything, go back to bed, and scout around in the morning."

"How are we supposed to go back to sleep knowing that thing might come back and rip our arms off like chicken wings?" Carter asked.

Angelo held out his notebook. "There are no documented attacks of a Bigfoot on a human. They do their best to avoid us."

"And I want to do my best to avoid them," Carter said.

Nick looked down at the footprint. A real Sasquatch

45

print. "If we did get it on film, would we be famous?"

Angelo grinned. "Are you kidding? They'd probably name a museum after us or something."

Carter sniffed. "I'd rather have a fast-food place named after me. Carter's Burgers and Shakes. Home of the Gargantuan Burger." He took the cookie package from Nick and looked inside with a disgusted frown. "Bigfoot is a total pig. It didn't leave a single crumb behind."

"Sounds like someone I know," Nick said. He gave one last look at the footprint and nodded. "Okay, let's do it."

Shivering in his sleeping bag, Nick was sure he would be awake all night. Every time a twig cracked outside or a gust of wind rattled the tent, he sat up, convinced he was about to be devoured. It wasn't until he heard Carter say, "What's that amazing smell?" that he realized he had fallen asleep.

Although the air was still cold, morning sunlight filtered through the trees, making shadows on the roof of the tent.

"At least we made it through the night without getting eaten by any Bigfeet," Nick said, unzipping his sleeping bag.

46

Angelo began grabbing equipment from his duffel bag and stuffing it into his backpack. "Actually, the plural of Bigfoot is still Bigfoot, not Bigfeet. And I told you, Bigfoot don't eat humans."

Maybe that was true, but Nick didn't want to be the first person to disprove the theory through personal experience.

Carter pulled on his shoes. "Speaking of eating, I'm almost sure I smell pancakes."

"The fluffiest pancakes this side of Broken Nose, Minnesota," a voice called out.

Nick unzipped the tent door to see his dad sitting in front of the camp stove beside a crackling fire. He was wearing an apron that read, "Don't Kiss the Cook. Like Him on Facebook."

"What's so special about Broken Nose, Minnesota?" Carter asked as he climbed out of the tent.

Nick winced—knowing his dad was about to launch into one of his crazy stories.

"Why, it's only the home of the fluffiest pancakes in the world!" Dad said. "It's a special combination of the latitude, the water, and a secret ingredient no one from the outside has yet discovered. But the batter is so light they actually used it in building the space shuttle."

Angelo wrinkled his nose. "There aren't any

47

pancakes in the space shuttle."

"Well, not anymore. That's why the space program is in such bad shape." Dad lifted a pancake from the griddle with his spatula and flipped it into the air. The pancake flew over his head, hit a tree branch, and landed in the dirt behind him. He shook his head wistfully. "Definitely not space shuttle material."

Mom climbed out of the tent and took the spatula. "Why don't I finish the pancakes while you get the plates and silverware out of the car?"

"Keep a close eye on them," Dad said. "They're culinary masterpieces." Pulling his keys from his pocket, he winked at the boys. "Don't think we didn't hear you three trying to get into the car last night."

Nick shot a quick glance at his friends. His parents had heard the Bigfoot too. Angelo gave a slight shake of his head. It wasn't obvious enough for Nick's parents to see, but Nick got the message. They couldn't let Mom and Dad know what had really made the noises. "Uhh, yeah. We were kind of hungry."

Dad tapped his head. "I expected that. But the old man was too smart for you. I locked the car before we went to bed."

"You couldn't have," Carter blurted. But Angelo put a finger to his lips.

Nick followed his father to the car. Sure enough, the doors were all locked.

"I was a boy once too," Dad said as he opened the back of the car and began grabbing plastic forks and paper plates. "There wasn't a place your grandmother hid sweets where I couldn't find them. Of course back then we didn't have the kind of candy you boys do now. We were lucky if we got honey-coated chicken gizzards."

"Don't believe him," Mom called, turning the pancakes. "When I married him he'd never seen a candy bar he didn't like."

"I'd try a honey-coated gizzard," Carter said. "Especially if it was on a pizza."

Nick pulled Angelo away toward the trees. "If the car was locked, how did the creature get the Oreos and gummy worms?"

Angelo lowered his head in thought. "Maybe your dad missed one of the doors?"

"And what, Bigfoot locked it after he got done stealing the food? I checked the car just now and they were all locked. Even the windows were open only an inch or so. There's no way anything could get inside." There was definitely something weird going on.

"Let's eat," Dad said. Juggling cups, plates, plastic

utensils, syrup, and a carton of orange juice, he started back toward the campfire. Halfway there, he began to lose his grip. Nick and Carter darted forward just as everything began to fall. Nick grabbed the plates and cups while Carter snagged the juice and made a diving grab for the syrup.

"Good catch," Dad said.

Carter grinned. "I'd give my life for syrup."

Mom dished scrambled eggs and pancakes onto everyone's plates. "We thought we'd head down to the beach right after breakfast."

"Actually, we were kind of hoping we could explore around here for a couple of hours," Nick said. He quickly turned to his father. "You know, because this is such an amazing campground you found."

Dad beamed. "I can't take *all* the credit. I mean, I *was* the one who saw the sign. And I *did* keep going when everyone else wanted to turn back. But other than that it was nothing anyone else wouldn't have done."

Mom stared into the woods. "I don't know. I don't like the idea of you boys wandering around by yourselves. You could get lost." She pressed her lips together. "Maybe if your dad went with you."

"No need," Angelo said at once. He reached into his pack and pulled out what looked like a handheld

video game system. "I brought a GPS. We couldn't get lost if we tried. I also brought a compass, a map of the woods, whistles in case of emergency, and a seventy-two-hour kit."

Mom looked impressed. "Maybe we'll have you pack for all of us from now on. And make the reservations."

Ignoring her jab, Dad waved toward the trees. "Have a good time, boys, but be back in two hours. Who knows, maybe you'll discover a new species out there."

Eating the last of his eggs, Nick thought, *As long as it doesn't discover us first.*

CHAPTER 7

HANSEL AND GRETEL SHOULD HAVE TRIED COOKIES

TRIED COOKIES

"That was a close one," Carter said as they hiked through the forest.

"No kidding," Angelo said. "As much as Nick's dad talks, we'd have zero chance of sneaking up on anything."

Nick tried to act offended. But the truth was his dad did talk a lot. "At least if we found something dangerous, he could put it to sleep with one of his stories." He looked at Angelo's bulging pack. "Do you really have all the stuff you said in there?"

Angelo pushed a few buttons on his GPS and nodded. "That and a lot more. I didn't mention the remote-controlled video recorder, DNA-collection kit, or digital binoculars."

Nick snorted. "You know, most people bring things like fishing poles and Frisbees on camping trips."

"Which is why most people never bring back any actual evidence when they come across a Sasquatch." Angelo knelt to the ground, examined the terrain, and pulled out his binoculars. "What we have to figure out is which direction to go."

"This way," Carter said from about twenty feet to their left.

"How could you possibly know that?" Angelo asked.

Carter placed a finger against the side of his head and gave a thoughtful pose. "Follow the evidence, young Padawan," he said around a mouthful of food.

Angelo gave him a scornful look. "What kind of evidence?"

"What's that you're eating?" Nick asked. "I thought all your snacks were back in the car."

"Oreos," Carter said. He ran about twenty yards ahead and picked something up. "There's a trail of them." He brushed the dirt off a cookie and popped it into his mouth.

Angelo raced to the spot and stared at Carter. "You've been following a trail of cookies since we left the camp?"

"A couple of them looked a little chewed on." Carter grinned—his teeth black with chewed-up Oreos. "But they taste just fine. Bigfoot don't have germs, do they?"

Angelo put his hands on his head. "You're eating evidence! And you didn't take pictures."

"It's an Oreo," Carter said, licking a crumb from his finger. "You want a picture of it, go into any grocery store."

"None of this makes sense," Nick said. "First, a monster breaks into a locked car without leaving any marks. Then, instead of rummaging through everything, it picks out gummy worms and a package of Oreos, which it carefully leaves a trail of for us to follow. Does this sound like anything you've seen in your Bigfoot research?"

Angelo wrote furiously in his notebook. "We're obviously dealing with a very intelligent being."

Nick watched Carter searching for the next cookie. "Intelligent enough to set a trap?"

Carter stopped. "Say what?"

"Think about it," Nick said. "We've invaded its territory. If it's smart enough to break into a locked car, couldn't it also be smart enough to lead us into a trap? One minute we're following a trail of Oreos. The next minute we're falling into a pit filled with sharp sticks or

getting smashed by a boulder poised to roll down on us the minute we step on the wrong spot."

Angelo chewed his lower lip. "We don't know very much about their species. But the fact that they've managed to stay undiscovered this long does suggest a rather high IQ."

Carter stood with one foot frozen in midair. "You couldn't have thought about this *before* I started following the trail?"

"That's assuming it didn't put anything *on* the cookies," Angelo said. "If it really wanted to get rid of us, it could coat them with an odorless, tasteless poison."

Carter groaned. "My stomach feels kind of weird."

"It couldn't have anything to do with the fact that you ate about thirty pancakes," Nick said. "If Bigfoot wanted to poison us, it could have put something in our food when it broke into the car."

"You think it poisoned the pancakes too?" Carter asked, his eyes wide. "The cookies *and* the pancakes? I'm a goner for sure."

"It didn't poison anything," Nick said. "The question is, why did it leave a trail for us and what do we do about it?"

Angelo rubbed his chin. "I say we follow the trail. But take precautions."

"What kind of precautions?" Nick asked.

"Here," Angelo said, taking a rope from his backpack. "We'll tie this to each other. If one of us steps on some kind of trap, the other two can save him."

"Or get pulled into the trap with him," Carter said. "No offense, but if I see some big, hairy ape-man, the last thing I want is a rope tied to me."

"Carter's right," Nick said. "It would be easy to get tangled on a tree or a bush if you have to move fast. Let's forget the rope and spread out—one of us in the middle and one to each side. That way, if one of us sets off a trap all three of us won't be caught in it."

"I'm not walking in the middle," Carter said. "I already tested the food for poison."

"I'd walk in the middle. But I have the GPS," Angelo said. "Someone has to lead us back in case of an emergency."

"Some monster hunters you guys are," Nick said. "Fine. I'll walk in the middle. But give me the video camera. If I'm going to track the Bigfoot, I want to be the one recording anything we see."

Angelo unzipped a pocket of his pack and took out a thin black rectangle attached to a Velcro strap. "You wear it on your head, so it sees whatever you see. This is the remote. Anytime you want to record, just push

the red button. You have a total of ninety minutes of recording time, but only push the button if you see something."

Nick's hair felt damp with sweat as he secured the camera to his head. He couldn't help thinking about all the movies where a kid is walking through the woods with a video camera and something jumps out of the trees. Suddenly the camera angle goes crazy and all you can hear is pounding footsteps and screams. He really didn't want his last words to be "What is that? No. No!"

"Here," Angelo said, handing them each a whistle. "If you see anything dangerous, blow this."

Nick hung the whistle around his neck. Taking a deep breath, he started farther into the woods. With the thick canopy of tree branches overhead it was almost like night. He looked left and right, searching for any sign of movement. But would he see something before it attacked? For all he knew, Bigfoot were masters of camouflage. He might not even know something was there until—

A branch cracked to his left, and Nick nearly screamed. His sweaty finger pressed at the record button as he spun around. It was only Carter. "Geez, you scared me to death," he whispered. "I thought we were going to spread out."

"I want to cover you if something attacks," Carter whispered back. "Besides, I was getting kind of freaked out all by myself."

"I know what you mean," Angelo said, joining them. "It feels like something's out there watching us."

"Yeah," Nick said. Every time he turned his head he had the strongest feeling that some creature had slipped back into the shadows just before he could see it. It might be safer to spread out, but he had to admit he felt more comfortable with his friends beside him. "What's the difference between a Bigfoot and a Sasquatch anyway?" he asked.

"Just different names," Angelo said, appearing relieved to be explaining something. "Sasquatch comes from the Native American language known as Salish. It means 'hairy giant.' Another tribe, the Lummi, called the creatures Ts'emekwes. 'Bigfoot' wasn't used until the late 1950s, when a bulldozer operator in Northern California discovered huge footprints. The first Bigfoot hunters appeared shortly after that."

"So the Bigfoot have been around for a long time?"

"Some people believe the original Bigfoot was a giant ape called Gigantopithecus that lived as much as nine million years ago."

Nick felt his mouth go dry. "That would explain

58

why they view us as intruders."

"Look." Carter pointed to the ground a few feet ahead.

As they got closer Nick saw another Oreo. A second later he realized it wasn't just one cookie, but several of them spread out on the ground. "What is it?" Nick asked.

"It's a bunch of cookies," Carter said, "and I'm starving." He reached for the Oreos but Angelo stopped him.

"Don't touch them," Angelo said. The cookies were arranged in three straight lines. He turned to Nick. "This can't be accidental. And look, there are more of the giant footprints. Are you recording this?"

Nick nodded, before remembering the camera was attached to his head. He stared straight down at the footprints and then moved his head toward the cookies to get a clear shot. "It's some kind of symbol. Any idea what it means?"

Angelo's jaw was set in concentration. "The Roman numeral three? Three people? Three is a special number for many groups. But in this case, I'm not sure."

"Maybe it's a warning." Nick glanced around, remembering the possibility of a trap. "Do you think we should spread out again? I don't see tripwires or anything, but . . ." He paused, staring at an especially large

redwood tree a few yards beyond the cookies. "Look at that," he said.

Angelo and Nick walked up to the tree, which was so big the three of them couldn't have reached around the trunk even if they all linked hands. The same three-line symbol was carved into the trunk, one on the left, one on the right, and one sideways about ten feet above the ground.

Angelo ran his fingers across the symbols.

"What is it?" Nick asked.

"It's a bunch of cookies," Carter said.

"Very funny," Nick said, gritting his teeth. Sometimes Carter could be so focused on food he forgot about everything else. "Do we keep going or search around here?"

Angelo scratched his head. "There has to be a reason for the symbol. It could be trying to tell us something."

"I'm hungry," Carter said.

Nick spun around to glare at him. "Can't you ever think about anything but your stomach?"

Carter's face was nearly as white as his hair. "I didn't say that."

"What are you talking about?" Angelo snapped, clearly as annoyed as Nick.

Carter raised a shaking hand to his face. "I didn't

say I was hungry. I mean, it was my voice. But I didn't say it."

Nick folded his arms across his chest, as if he could somehow hold back his anger. "If you didn't say you were hungry, who did?"

His hand still shaking, Carter pointed behind the redwood tree. "H-he did."

Nick leaned far enough left to look behind the tree and froze. Standing in the shadows looking back at him was an exact duplicate of Carter. The duplicate was a perfect copy, all the way down to the black hair with the white stripe. It could have been Carter's twin except for the fact that it was only six inches tall.

The tiny Carter look-alike grinned up at the three boys and rubbed its stomach. "I'm hungry."

Carter blew his whistle.

CHAPTER 8

MAYBE NICK'S FATHER SHOULD HAVE PAID MORE ATTENTION IN HIS GERMAN CLASS

Tweet. Twee-ee-eet. Tweeeeeeeeet!

The ear-piercing sound of Carter's repeated whistles drilled into Nick's head like a sharp spike. "Would you cut that out?" he yelled, covering his ears.

"What is it?" Carter cried around the whistle still jammed between his lips. "It l-looks j-just like me."

If the whistles and shouting bothered the tiny Carter, it didn't show it. "It l-looks j-just like me," it repeated in such a perfect copy of Carter's voice that it could have been a recording.

For one of the few times Nick had ever seen, Angelo appeared to be at a complete loss for words. He knelt in front of the tiny figure, twisted his monster notebook in his hands, and muttered, "Huh."

"That's it?" Carter said. "'Huh'? That's all you have to say? What is that thing and why does it look like me?"

"It doesn't just look *like* you," Nick said. "It looks *exactly* like you. It sounds exactly like you. It has the same clothes as you. It even has a tiny little syrup stain on its shirt like you."

"I can see that." Carter stumbled backward a couple of steps, and his miniature double followed him.

Angelo shook his head, like a boxer recovering from an especially hard punch. "I . . . I think it could be a homunculus."

"A hom-what-what?" Nick asked. Around them, the birds that had gone silent at the sound of Carter's whistle started up their singing again.

Angelo flipped through his notebook, shaking his head. "I didn't think they were real until this minute." He finally found the page he was looking for, reading his notes out loud. "Homunculus. Latin for 'little man.' First spoken of in alchemical writings of the sixteenth century. Said to be a perfect replica of a human being in miniature form."

"That's what it looks like all right," Nick said.

Carter backed away again and picked up a stick. "Is it dangerous?"

The homunculus followed, picking up a twig of its own.

"Nothing I've read says they are," Angelo said. "In fact some writings refer to them as symbols of purity and innocence."

Slowly, Carter put down his stick. The homunculus put down its twig and in a perfect Carter voice said, "I'm hungry."

"It even acts like you," Nick said with a laugh.

Carter reached into his pocket and pulled out a couple of Skittles. He tossed one to the miniature him. It picked up the candy in its tiny hands, sniffed it, and took a big bite. "Yum!"

Carter grinned. "It likes it!"

"How could anything that looks this much like you not like candy?" Nick asked.

The homunculus finished its Skittle and looked up at Carter. "Want another Skittle?" Carter asked, holding out his hand.

The creature tilted its head and for a moment, Nick didn't think it would come any closer. Then it rubbed its stomach, hopped up into Carter's hand, and took the candy. "Skittle," it repeated before chowing down.

Carter was delighted. "Look at this."

Nick stepped back and motioned Angelo to join

him. "Are you sure it's safe?" he whispered.

"I don't know anything about it," Angelo admitted with a shrug. "But it doesn't *seem* dangerous."

That wasn't exactly the most comforting thing Nick could have heard. Bears looked cuddly too—until they ripped your face off. For all the boys knew, it could have rabies or something. "Maybe you should put it down," he said.

But Carter wasn't paying any attention. He slipped the homunculus into his jacket pocket and it popped out a moment later with a sunflower seed gripped in its hands. "I didn't know I had that in there," Carter laughed.

Angelo watched, fascinated.

"Do you know where it came from?" Nick asked.

Angelo waved his notebook excitedly in the air. "I don't have enough data. As far as I'm aware, no one's ever reported an actual sighting."

"Watch this," Carter said. He tapped the first two fingers of his left hand against his right palm. The homunculus did a little jig in his hand. "I taught it to dance." He patted his pockets. "Do you want some more candy?"

The little Carter frowned and said, "If it was a raccoon, I'm turning it into a coonskin cap."

Carter burst into laughter. But Nick got an uneasy feeling in his stomach. "Did you hear that?" he asked. "It just repeated what Carter said last night outside the tent. It must have been spying on us."

"He wouldn't spy," Carter said, feeding the homunculus a crumb of potato chip. "Would you, little guy?"

"It's probably the one who broke into our car too," Nick mused. He didn't care if Angelo said the homunculus was dangerous or not. He had a bad feeling about it.

Carter held out his hand. "Let's see you dance again, little me."

The homunculus's dancing was interrupted by a car's horn honking from the direction of the camp. Nick checked his watch. They'd been gone for only a little over thirty minutes. "I wonder what's up."

"You think we're in trouble?" Angelo asked.

"I don't see how we could be," Nick said. "Dad told us we could stay out for two hours, and it hasn't been half that yet."

The car honked again.

"Whatever it is, we better get back," Nick told his friends.

Carter tucked the homunculus into the crook of his arm, where it curled up like a baby, before joining Nick and Angelo.

66

"What are you doing?" Nick asked. "You can't bring that with you."

"Why not? It likes me. Besides, do you have any idea how much people will pay to see a tiny human dancing and talking? I'm gonna be rich." Carter lightly rubbed the top of the homunculus's head and it sighed contentedly.

Nick turned to Angelo. "Tell him he can't take that thing with him. We have no idea what kinds of diseases it might have."

Carter scowled at him. "Carter Junior does not have any diseases."

"It might be better if you left it here," Angelo said. "We don't know its environmental needs. There could be something special about this habitat. It might be the only place it can survive. Even though it looks like a human, it's actually a wild animal."

Carter narrowed his eyes. "Who are you calling an animal?"

"It could get sick," Angelo said. "And besides, if you start showing that thing around, people are going to want to do tests on it. Or put it in a zoo. How would you feel about that?"

Carter tightened his jaw. "You're just mad that it doesn't look like you." He lowered the homunculus to

the ground and gave it a piece of beef jerky.

"I'm hungry," the homunculus said.

Carter wiped his eyes. "I'm gonna miss you. Be careful, and stay away from those Oreos. A little guy like you will balloon up in no time from all the cream filling."

The car honked a third time—an urgent *beep-beep-beep-beeeep.*

"Let's go," Nick said.

"Go ahead," Carter said. "I'll catch up with you. I just want to say good-bye."

Nick rolled his eyes, then nodded. "Okay. But hurry. It sounds like my parents really want us back there." He and Angelo started back toward the camp. A moment later, Carter joined them and the three boys raced back through the woods with Angelo checking his GPS to keep them going in the right direction.

When they reached the camp, Mom was standing by the fire pit searching anxiously for them. "Where have you been?" she asked. "I've been honking for fifteen minutes."

Nick looked around the camp. The tents, sleeping bags, and stove were all back in the car. "What's going on?" he asked. "Dad said we could have two hours to explore."

Mom waved a hand toward the gravel parking lot, where Dad was talking to a man in a floppy gray hat and a green plaid coat. Actually, there wasn't much talking going on. The man in the gray hat was shouting and Dad was mostly just nodding.

"Apparently this isn't a campground after all. It seems we've been trespassing on private property and the owner, Mr. Grunwald, is not very happy about it."

"He sure isn't," Nick said. From what he could see, the man looked like he was going to give himself a heart attack if he didn't calm down.

"*Heiliger Bimbam!*" the man shouted. "Are you not reading the sign?"

"It's in German," Nick's dad said. "I thought it said something about camping."

"*Sapperlot!*" the man screamed. He threw his hat to the ground and straightened the sign, revealing the English translation that had been hidden when Nick's dad knocked it into the trees. DANGER! STAY AWAY! NOT CAMPSITE! NO HIKING, FISHING, OR HUNTING!

"Guess we missed that," Dad said. He pulled out his wallet. "I'd be happy to pay."

"*Nein!*" the man yelled, his face nearly purple with rage. He spun around and spotted Nick and his friends. "You. *Jungen.* You touch nothing?"

Nick glanced nervously at Carter and Angelo. "Um, no. We didn't touch anything."

The man marched up to them, his hands clenched. For a second Nick thought the man was going to hit him. Instead, he pointed into the trees. His bushy gray eyebrows pulled so low that his eyes nearly disappeared. He turned to Angelo. "You boys are seeing something in forest?"

"No," Angelo said at once. "We were just bird-watching." He pulled the binoculars out of his pack. "See? For birds."

"Birds." The man took a handkerchief from his coat pocket and honked his bulbous red nose into it. He glared at Carter. "You are touching nothing? Taking nothing?"

Carter gulped, his Adam's apple bobbing up and down. He folded his hands behind his back. "No. I, um, didn't take anything."

"Come on now," Dad said, stepping between the man and the boys. "It was an honest mistake. So the actual campground was off the next exit. Is there really any harm done? I offered to pay you for the inconvenience."

The man wheeled around. "Out!" he shouted. "Out and never coming back!"

As quickly as they could, Nick, his friends, and his parents piled into the car and drove down the road. Standing in a cloud of dust behind them, the man continued to shout and wave his fists.

Angelo leaned over to Nick and whispered, "Well, your dad was right about it being an adventure."

CHAPTER 9

WHEN SOMEONE TELLS YOU THEY HAVE A LITTLE PROBLEM, ALWAYS ASK, "*HOW* LITTLE?"

The ride home was not a happy one. Dad drove with his jaw set and his eyes locked on the road ahead. For once it was Mom trying to crack jokes.

"The good news is we have plenty of supplies left over. You really can't have too much dehydrated camping food."

Nick tried to smile but he was still a little freaked out by the homunculus and the odd German man's reaction to them being on his property. "That guy sure was mad."

"Oh, I don't know," Mom said. "When he wasn't screaming, throwing his hat, or spouting incomprehensible German phrases, he seemed rather friendly."

"He was screaming the whole time," Carter said.

Angelo elbowed him. "It was a joke."

"Oh." Carter laughed weakly. "Good one, Mrs. B."

A stop for fast food didn't lighten the mood either. No one seemed to have much of an appetite. Even Carter took only a bite or two of his hamburger before tucking the rest of it into his backpack.

"You might as well throw that out," Nick said. "It's just going to go bad."

Carter shrugged, and looked away. "I might get hungry again in a little while."

Nick studied him. "Are you okay? You look a little weird."

Carter's cheeks turned pink. "It's just . . . you know."

"Yeah." Nick patted him on the shoulder. "I'm sorry you had to leave it behind."

"Leave what behind?" Mom asked.

Angelo looked quickly up from his notebook. "The campground. Carter was sad to leave it."

"Right," Carter said. "I was really getting attached to the great outdoors."

Dad muttered something under his breath and Mom laid a hand on the back of his neck. "It's probably a good thing we got out when we did. I heard the weather was getting ready to turn bad."

Nick looked out the window. The sky was blue and clear. "Yeah. It was feeling kind of chilly this morning. Might be a storm coming in."

Dad gritted his teeth. "The only clouds around here are the ones I caused by ruining our trip."

After that, no one even tried to talk to him. Mom opened a paperback. Angelo studied his monster notebook, occasionally jotting down a note or two. Carter kept acting weird, fiddling with his backpack and saying nothing.

Nick stared out the car window, trying to make sense of what they'd seen. The appearance of the homunculus and the reaction of the German man had to be related. Did the guy know what was on his property? Nick thought he probably did. Which meant what? Was it some kind of sanctuary where the creatures lived?

What kept the creatures from leaving? Unless maybe they did leave sometimes. That brought up another question he hadn't even considered. He made sure his mother was still reading and leaned over to Carter. "Remember when you threw up yesterday?"

"How could I forget?" Carter said. "It was a waste of perfectly good beef jerky and a full bag of corn nuts."

"I don't want to know the contents of your stomach. I was just thinking about the voice you said you heard."

74

Carter blinked. "What about it?"

"Well, the spot where you yakked was pretty close to where we pulled off to camp last night. You think the voice you heard on the side of the road could have been another homunculus? Or even the same one?"

Carter looked down at his pack, strangely subdued. "Maybe."

"I guess it doesn't really matter," Nick said. "I was just thinking that it's weird no one has ever seen a homunculus before. Especially with a freeway so close by. Maybe what Angelo said about their habitat was right. That might be the only place they can live."

Carter frowned. "Or maybe no one ever gave them a chance to try living anywhere else."

Nick guessed that was a possibility too. "We'll probably never know."

As soon as they got home, Carter and Angelo grabbed their things out of the car.

"I'm going to do some more research," Angelo said before heading home. "For now I say we all stay quiet about what we saw."

"Definitely," Nick said. "If people knew there was a homunculus, or maybe a bunch of them up there, they'd never leave them alone."

Carter clutched his pack awkwardly in front of him.

"See you guys tomorrow."

After helping his mom and dad unpack, Nick showered and finished a homework assignment that was due the next day. Sometime around nine, he made himself a PB and J sandwich and went to bed. For something that was supposed to be restful, camping was exhausting.

Nick was hoping that by Monday morning everything would be back to normal. But when he walked into the kitchen, his mother and father were sitting silently across the table from each other, staring into their coffee cups.

"Everything okay?" Nick asked, pouring himself a bowl of cereal.

Dad slurped his drink without saying a word.

"Your father's still pouting about the camping trip," Mom finally said.

Dad set his mug down with a *bang*, splashing coffee on the kitchen table. "I'm not pouting."

"You haven't said ten words since we got back and all you've done is frown and watch the Outdoor Channel. What would you call that?"

Nick swallowed a mouthful of Frosted Flakes. "At least the tents didn't blow down a hill this time."

Apparently that was the wrong thing to say. Dad pushed back his chair and burst from the table. "Fine! I'm the worst outdoorsman ever. Next year we'll stay in a hotel and order room service."

"I didn't mean—" Nick started, but his dad was already out the door that lead to the garage.

"Give him a little time," Mom said. "Before you know it, he'll be planning the next big adventure."

"It really wasn't that bad," Nick said. "In fact, parts of the trip were a little *too* exciting."

Mom laughed. "No one ever said your father was boring."

As Nick got up to rinse his bowl, Angelo bounded through the back door. "I've been doing some more research and—" He spotted Nick's mom and paused. "Uh, hi, Mrs. Braithwaite."

"Monster talk?" Mom gave a wry smile and picked up her mug. "You know, if I'd had a daughter I wouldn't have to hear about werewolves, vampires, and mummies every waking minute."

"I wouldn't be so sure," Nick said. "Angie is a girl and she and her friends love monsters almost as much as we do."

As soon as Nick's mom was out of the kitchen, Angelo sat down at the table. "All right, I've been doing

some reading. What we saw could be a homunculus. But it could also be an imp, a brownie, or even some kind of fairy."

Nick laughed. "A fairy that looks and eats like Carter? Now *that* is a nightmare creature. So which one is it?"

Angelo shook his head. "There's no way to know for sure. I'm guessing homunculus, though."

"But how would it get there? Where do they come from?"

"Nobody seems to know for sure," Angelo said. "But there are two schools of thought. Some people think they are scientifically created."

Nick shivered, remembering Dr. Dippel and everything that had happened when the boys had explored his haunted school with Angie, Dana, and Tiffany a few weeks earlier. "You think that German guy was some kind of scientist, creating little people in a secret lab?"

"If he was, where was his laboratory? And why wasn't there a fence or something to keep people from discovering his creations? It seems strange that he would have such lax security."

That was the great thing about having a friend like Angelo. He considered every angle.

"Okay," Nick said. "So if they aren't created in a lab,

where *do* they come from?"

Angelo flipped open his notebook. "There's no definitive proof. But according to folklore, homunculi are closely related to small, beardless, humanlike beings called *mandragora*, or, as the Germans call them, *alreona*."

"Mandragora, I think I've heard of those," Nick said. "Don't they come from plants or something?"

"Mandrake plants, to be precise," Angelo said. He pointed to a picture of a flat plant with thick, dark green leaves. "They grow a long, wrinkled root that can look nearly human. Supposedly, if you pick them at the right time they form actual little people. You have to cover your ears to protect yourself from their screams or they can kill you."

"And these mandrake plants grow here?" Nick asked.

"Not usually. The plants are native to western Europe. But from everything I've read, if you have the right soil and the right temperature, they *can* grow here. Or this one could come from some other kind of plant."

That made sense. The guy who'd kicked them off his property seemed much more like an angry farmer who'd found someone trespassing in his garden than like a mad scientist. But there was still the part that had

bothered him ever since the drive home. "If that guy is growing homunculi, why would he let them roam free? Couldn't they end up wandering onto the highway and getting hit by a car?"

"Maybe not," Angelo said. "This is just a hunch. But if they are related to the mandragoras, it's entirely possible that they can't survive long away from where they were originally grown."

"Oh, no," a voice said.

Nick and Angelo turned to see Carter standing by the kitchen door. Neither of them had heard him come in. He clutched his backpack to his chest and something moved inside it.

Nick put his hand to his mouth. "Tell me that isn't what I think it is in there."

Carter bit his lip and looked away. "Guys, we might have a little problem."

CHAPTER 10

YOU HAVE TO ADMIT, IT'S A MUCH BETTER PET THAN ONE OF THOSE YAPPY LITTLE DOGS WITH A NAME YOU CAN'T PRONOUNCE

"How could you do it?" Angelo demanded, his eyes blazing behind his thick glasses. "We specifically told you to leave the homunculus in the woods. Don't you realize you could make it sick or even kill it by taking it out of its natural habitat?"

Carter scratched at the white stripe down the middle of his hair and hung his head. "I was planning to let him go. Really. But then he looked up at me with those sad little eyes of mine—I mean his—and I thought, what if by feeding him we made it so he can't survive on his own? How would I feel if I did something to hurt the little guy?"

Nick was so mad he could feel his pulse pounding in

his head. "So you thought you'd just bring it home and what? Make a pet out of it? Where did you think you were going to keep it, a hamster cage?"

"I didn't think about any of that!" Carter shouted. "I just opened my pack and he climbed in."

Mom stuck her head into the kitchen. "Everything okay in here?"

"We're fine," Nick said, shooting Carter a dark look. "Carter was just telling us about a movie where a dumb kid brings home a wild animal and learns what a bad idea that is."

"Well, you better get out the door or you're going to be late."

Glaring at one another, the three boys walked out the door and started toward school. As soon as they were out of sight of the house, Carter turned to Nick. "I'm planning on taking Carter Junior back, okay? I knew it was a bad idea to take him as soon as I got to the campsite. But by then that guy was screaming at us and I was afraid to let him see what I'd done." He looked down at the backpack, which was wriggling more and more. "The thing is, I think there's something wrong with him."

Angelo stepped forward. "What do you mean? Is it sick?"

Carter's pack shook and a little voice called out, "Is it sick?"

Nick stared at Angelo. Angelo stared at Carter. Carter stared down at the pack. Slowly he unzipped the back pocket and a tiny head popped out. It rubbed its glasses, looked owlishly at the boys, and said in an all-too-familiar voice, "It's entirely possible that they can't survive long away from where they were originally grown."

It was a little Angelo.

Angelo blinked at the miniature version of himself. The little Angelo blinked back at him. "It's . . . it's me."

Nick couldn't help laughing. "It looks exactly like you. It even has a tiny monster notebook."

Carter gulped. "That's what I've been trying to tell you guys. It keeps changing. First it was me. Then it was Angelo. Then—"

"It looks exactly like you," the tiny Angelo said. Except it wasn't Angelo anymore. So quickly Nick hadn't seen it happen, the homunculus had turned into a copy of him.

The mini Nick put its hands on its hips, frowned, and growled, "Where did you think you were going to keep it, a hamster cage?"

He gawked at the little him. "That doesn't sound like me."

83

"It really does," Angelo said. "It looks like you too. All the way to the hair sticking up in the back."

"That doesn't sound like me," the homunculus said in Nick's voice. Instantly it changed back to Angelo. "It really does," it said in Angelo's voice. "It looks like you too."

Angelo flipped open his notebook. "When did this start?"

"Last night. About an hour after I got home." Carter patted the homunculus's head. "I was sitting in my room, trying to figure out what to do, when Carter Junior changed into Angelo. At first it was kind of funny. He sounded just like you. 'Technically, the statistics point to a probability of—'"

"Technically, the statistics point to a probability of," the homunculus said, waving its monster notebook theatrically in a perfect imitation of Angelo lecturing.

Carter looked down at it, his face a mask of worry and guilt. "Do you think I did something to him? He's still eating and sleeping. But the changes have been coming faster and faster."

Angelo's brow wrinkled in concentration. "It's possible this is normal behavior. Or even a stage of development. But there's no way of knowing. We've got to return it to its home as soon as possible."

84

Nick glanced at his watch. "Not to break up the party, guys, but if we don't book it now we're gonna be tardy."

"Book it," the homunculus said in Nick's voice. "Do you think I did something?" it said, changing into Carter.

Angelo sighed. "We can't take it to school like that."

"I can keep him quiet," Carter said. "He really likes black licorice and playing with my Nintendo DS. If I turn the sound off and sneak him food, no one will even know he's there."

Nick and Angelo shared a concerned look.

"I can't leave him home," Carter said. "And if I miss one more day of school before the end of the semester, I'll get suspended."

There didn't appear to be much choice. "All right," Nick said. "We'll take him to school. But you have to make sure *nobody* sees him."

Running the whole way, they managed to get to class just before the bell rang. As they came through the door, Angie Hollingsworth and her friends Dana and Tiffany were waiting. The girls considered themselves at least as knowledgeable about monsters as Nick, Angelo, and Carter. The two groups had been archenemies until recently, when they'd had to work

together to save another student from an evil mad scientist. Now there was a kind of truce that no one seemed completely comfortable with.

"Look who's here," Angie said with a smirk. "I guess I lose a chocolate cupcake."

Nick raised a single eyebrow—something he'd been working on over the past few weeks. "Do I even want to know why?"

Angie flipped back her red hair and grinned. "I bet Dana that at least one of you would get lost in the woods and they'd have to send out search-and-rescue."

"Nice to know you cared," Nick said, the sarcasm in his voice thicker than caramel on a banana split.

Carter pulled a piece of licorice out of his jacket, slipped it into his pack, and whispered something toward the back pocket.

"What's with him?" Dana asked.

Angelo's right eye twitched. "Uh, nothing." He looked toward the front corner of the room, where a group of girls were crowded around a desk. "What's going on over there?"

Tiffany sniffed. "Kimber Tidwell is such a twit. She's decided that hats and puffy skirts are now in fashion. Although where she came up with such a ridiculous idea, I have no clue. Not a single fashion designer has

said anything of the kind."

Tiffany was a nut about fashion trends. But Kimber had been the most popular girl in the school since kindergarten. Anything she and her friends Torrie and Rebel decided was cool suddenly became trendy whether Tiffany liked it or not.

"Take your seats, please," Ms. Schoepf said.

As Nick went to his desk, he mouthed to Carter, "Keep it hidden."

Carter gave a thumbs-up. But the homunculus was already squirming around in his backpack. It would be a miracle if someone didn't notice it—especially Angie and her friends, who had eagle eyes when it came to figuring out what the boys were up to.

Fortunately, Ms. Schoepf kept them all busy with a math test, a history pop quiz, and a long lecture on the importance of the semicolon. Even Nick didn't have time to think about the homunculus.

It wasn't until the lunch bell rang and the kids began heading out the door to the playground that he remembered to check on Carter.

"How's it going?" he asked.

"Not good," Carter whispered. "Carter Junior's been restless. I don't think the licorice agreed with his stomach."

"No kidding," Nick said. "Did it ever occur to you to try feeding it something healthy? Like, say, vegetables?"

"Vegetables are for rabbits and hamsters," Carter said.

"Keep your voices down," Angelo said. He glanced over at Kimber, Torrie, and Rebel, who were flouncing around in skirts that could have fit at least three girls each from what Nick could see.

"I'm telling you," Kimber told anyone who would listen. "Soon everyone will be wearing puffy skirts. It's going to be like polyester in the seventies."

"If you mean ugly, uncomfortable, and something you'll want to hide pictures of in the future, I'm sure you're right," Tiffany said.

Rebel lowered her sunglasses and peered out from under a floppy hat with a huge orange sunflower on the side. "Look. It's the wannabe patrol. Where's your I-wish-I-was-cool-too badge?"

Torrie spun around, making her pink skirt open like a carnation around her legs, and glared at Tiffany. "By the time the *masses* realize what's cool, we'll be wearing the next new thing."

"Just ignore them," Angie said. "They'd wear cardboard boxes if they thought it would get them attention."

88

"Trust me," Kimber said. "We'd look better in cardboard than you look in those . . ." She waved her hands at Angie's clothes. ". . . whatever you call that."

Angelo nodded toward the far corner of the schoolyard and whispered to Nick and Carter, "Let's get away from everyone else and get a look at the you-know-what."

Making sure no one was following them, the boys crossed the basketball courts and sat down beneath the shade of an old oak. Carter unzipped his pack and eased the homunculus out. "How are you feeling, little guy?"

Angelo studied the creature, which at the moment looked like Carter. "Its skin seems kind of green."

"Maybe we should try giving it medicine," Nick said.

Angelo immediately shook his head. "It would be impossible to know how it might react. Plus, how would you calculate the right dose?"

The homunculus clutched its stomach and moaned. It was pitiful to hear. "We can't just let him suffer," Carter said.

The three boys stared at the little creature, unsure of what to do. Before they could come up with a plan, the little Carter opened its mouth and let out a belch that echoed across the playground.

"Whoa," Carter said. "That was awesome, little dude. I guess it wasn't the licorice after all. Maybe I gave him too much Mountain Dew."

Angelo slapped a hand to his forehead. "You've been feeding him candy *and* soda? What were you thinking?"

Carter held out his hands, palms up. "I figured since he looked like me, he should probably eat like me."

The homunculus looked up and gave a wide grin. "I'm hungry."

"See," Carter said. "It takes one candy-aholic to know one."

"What *is* that?" a voice asked.

Nick and his friends turned to see Angie, Dana, and Tiffany standing right behind them.

CHAPTER 11

I ONCE LEFT MY PET TARANTULA'S CAGE OPEN. MY SISTER THOUGHT IT WAS A SCREAM

Nick immediately moved between the girls and the homunculus. "You were spying on us!"

"As if," Tiffany said, shaking out her dark hair.

"Why would we want to spy on *you*?" Dana asked.

"Then get lost," Nick said.

"We were coming to see if you were going to Monster Movie Madness Saturday at the mall," Angie said. "But we're not going anywhere until you tell us what you were doing with that doll."

"It's not a doll," Carter said as Angelo tried to hush him.

"It's not *anything*. Now scram," Nick hissed.

"It's not anything," a miniature Nick repeated,

jumping onto Nick's shoulder.

Angie's eyes went wide as the homunculus changed into a perfect copy of her, tilted its chin, and said, "I guess I lose a chocolate cupcake."

Carter's mouth swung open like a box on a hinge. "Carter Junior can turn into a girl?"

Angelo grabbed the creature. It glared up at him with a perfect Angie sneer and said, "I bet Dana that at least one of you would get lost in the woods and they'd have to send out search-and-rescue."

"It's alive." Angie stared at her tiny double. "Did you . . . *make* it somehow?"

Angelo shook his head. "We found it while we were camping."

"An imp?" Dana asked. "Or some type of fairy?"

"That's what I thought at first," Angelo said, pulling out his notebook. "But after more research I've come to the conclusion that it's either a homunculus or a mandragora."

"A tiny human," Dana whispered almost reverently. "Does anyone else know about it?"

"No," Nick said at once. "And we want to keep it that way. Do you have any idea what people would do if they found out we have this?"

"Found out you have what?" a voice asked snottily.

It was Kimber Tidwell. "Obviously not body odor. Because everyone knows you have that."

Rebel spotted the homunculus Angelo was still gripping. "He has a doll that looks just like Angie."

Torrie giggled. "Is she your girlfriend, brainiac? Even *you* can do better than that."

Before Angelo could stop it, the homunculus squirmed out of his grip and turned into Kimber. Waving its hands theatrically in the air, it said, "Soon everyone will be wearing puffy skirts." Instantly it changed into Torrie. "Even someone like you can do better than that."

Kimber pulled down her sunglasses. "How did it do that?"

"It's not a doll. It's alive." Rebel snatched for the homunculus, but it danced out of her reach, bunched up its fists, and, in a perfect impression of Tiffany's comment that morning, said, "Kimber Tidwell is such a twit."

Nick grabbed the creature. It twisted in his hands, but he refused to let go. "That's enough show-and-tell." He gave Angelo a desperate look and hid the homunculus behind his back. "If you girls want your own, check eBay."

"eBay?" Kimber asked. She moved around to get a

better look. But Angelo stepped in front of her.

"Right," Angelo said. "But good luck getting one. The technology prototypes are nearly impossible to find. Especially with the remote control and facial duplication feature. It takes some serious microprocessing power to pull that off."

Torrie took off her hat. "What are you talking about? Don't try to tell me that thing's some kind of robot. It moved and talked. It's real."

"Real impressive animatronics technology," Dana said. "I'm surprised you haven't heard of it. But then again, you three don't pay attention to that kind of stuff. You're too busy with princess dresses."

Tiffany laughed. "Maybe you should keep up with the trends."

Kimber's face went bright red. She spun around. "Come on. Let them play with their toys. They're too lame to have any *real* friends."

Torrie and Rebel followed her across the playground. But Rebel kept glancing over her shoulder. "I don't think it was a toy."

As soon as they were gone, Nick gave Carter the homunculus. "Put that thing away and make sure no one sees it."

Carter patted the creature, which seemed exhausted

by its performance. Wrapping it gently in what looked like a doll blanket, he put it inside his backpack. "Don't worry. I think it's going to sleep."

"What are you guys going to do with it?" Angie asked. "Please tell me burp breath isn't keeping it as a pet."

"We're returning it to its primary habitat as soon as possible," Angelo said. "And you three have to swear not to say anything about it."

Dana tugged at a strand of honey-colored hair. "We won't tell. But are you sure it's a good idea to take it back?"

Nick watched Carter put the homunculus to bed and realized that, just like his friend, he actually felt sort of protective of the little guy—or girl. "What else would we do with it?"

Dana twisted the strand of hair back and forth. "Who knows if it can live in the wild now that it's been around humans? Besides, it *is* an entirely new species. Scientists would go ape to learn more about it."

"You want to let people do tests on it?" Angelo asked.

"They wouldn't have to do tests," Angie said. "They could keep it somewhere safe and study it. Even put it on display."

Carter balled up his fists. "Nobody's doing tests on Carter Junior. And nobody's putting him in a zoo."

"Fine." Dana held up her hands. "I'm just saying we should at least give it a little thought before we decide anything."

"*We* aren't deciding anything," Nick growled. "Angelo, Carter, and I are taking Carter Junior back to where he belongs, and the three of you are pretending you never saw a thing."

Angelo tapped his notebook silently.

Angie nodded. "You three found it. You can do what you want with it. Come on," she said to Dana and Tiffany. "Let's finish our lunch before the bell rings."

"That was easy," Carter said. "I've never seen Angie give up on an argument that quickly."

"Maybe she realized it was the right thing to do," Angelo said.

"Maybe," Nick agreed. But part of him wondered if that was all there was to it.

That night, the three boys gathered at Carter's house. Carter lay on his bed reading a comic book. Spread out on Carter's chest, Carter Junior read a miniature version of the same comic.

Nick swept aside a potato chip bag and at least six

candy bar wrappers to sit on the floor by Carter's bed. "How do you live in this mess?"

Carter closed his book long enough to check the chip bag for crumbs. "Just fine, thanks."

Sitting at the desk, Angelo opened a brown paper bag and took out a couple of Tupperware containers. "I brought some food for the homunculus."

"Really?" Carter sat up, but wrinkled his nose and plopped back onto his pillow when Angelo opened the containers. "Fruits and vegetables? Yuck."

"I don't want you to feed it any more candy," Angelo said. "And no more soda either. From now on it's fruit, vegetables, and water."

Carter crossed his legs. "I can try. But I don't think he's going to go for that stuff. The little guy's got a serious sweet tooth."

Carter Junior crossed his legs. "Fruits and vegetables? Yuck."

Carter chuckled. "See?"

Angelo looked at the homunculus before signaling the other boys. "Can we, um, talk in private? Without you-know-who listening?"

"Sure." Carter lifted the miniature version of himself off his chest and set him on the floor. "Go get us some Cheetos."

"Cheetos," the homunculus repeated before trotting out the door.

"Is that safe?" Nick asked. "What if your family sees him?"

Carter brushed the idea away with a wave. "Mom and Dad are on a date, and my sisters wouldn't look away from the television if the house was on fire. Besides, I've trained Carter Junior to sneak around without being seen."

"Really?" Angelo jotted something in his notebook. "I wondered if it might be learning. If it is, that makes what I have to say even more important." He steepled his fingers in front of his chest, almost as if he was praying. "We have to assume the homunculus is capable of more than we think."

Nick felt something jabbing him in the back and pulled out a Popsicle stick from under the bed. "What do you mean?"

"I think it's doing more than learning about our food and our mannerisms—what we say, how we act. I think it understands *what* we're saying."

Carter searched under his pillow for a snack. "Of course he does. I've been teaching him all kinds of stuff. How to use the remote control and play video games. He's pretty good at *Need for Speed Most Wanted*."

Angelo nodded. "Which means it could know what we're planning."

Nick sat up straight, understanding dawning on him. "He knows we're planning on returning him to the forest?"

Angelo frowned. "And it's entirely possible the homunculus doesn't want to go back to a place where there won't be any more sugar, snacks, or video games."

"Are you saying we can keep him?" Carter asked.

"No. The homunculus is a wild creature." Angelo gave Carter a meaningful look. "Whether we like it or not, being removed from the wild is not good for it. However, we must at least consider the possibility that the creature may try to stop us from returning it to its home."

"Wow," Nick said. He checked the hallway to make sure the homunculus wasn't outside listening. "What should we do?"

Angelo got up from the desk. "I checked the bus schedule, and we can get dropped off at the exit where your dad got off the freeway. But getting there and back will be an all-day trip. We can't pull it off until this weekend."

He shut the bedroom door. "Until then, we need to keep it either where we can see it or locked up at all

times." He turned to Carter. "Do you have a cage or tank of some kind?"

Carter thought for a minute. "I have an aquarium I used to keep turtles in. I don't have the turtles. But I still have the aquarium in my closet."

Angelo walked to the bed and placed a hand on Carter's shoulder. "I know this might be difficult for you. But from now until Saturday, anytime you are sleeping, at school, or anywhere you can't see it, Carter Junior needs to be locked in the aquarium. And make sure you put something heavy over the top of the tank. I think the homunculus could be a lot stronger than he lets us see."

CHAPTER 12

DIDN'T WE ALL SEE THIS COMING?

Tuesday morning, Nick woke up early with a weird craving for chocolate-coated Cheetos. Either he'd been having bizarre dreams or Carter was rubbing off on him. Determined to resist the temptation, he reached for a box of Rice Chex for breakfast. But he hadn't even poured the milk when Carter himself came busting through the kitchen door, tennis shoes squeaking on the kitchen tiles as he raced across them.

"Is Angelo here?" he gasped, looking around wildly.

"No." Nick checked the clock on the wall. "And you shouldn't be either. School doesn't start for more than an hour."

Carter grabbed Nick's arm. "You have to help me before Angelo finds out."

Nick felt a ball of ice form in his gut as all thoughts of food disappeared. "Before Angelo finds out *what*?"

"Okay, here it is." Carter took a couple of deep breaths to steady himself and said, "Carter Junior is gone."

"Are you kidding me?" Nick leaped to his feet. "Didn't you put him in the aquarium?"

"Of course I did," Carter said, panting as if he'd run all the way from his house. "I put a little bed in there and water and vegetables just like Angelo said. I gave him the Nintendo DS, and a bag of Skittles to hold him over. I don't think he liked it when I put the board on top. But I did it anyway. I even put, like, ten pounds of books on top of the board."

Nick squeezed his hands together, trying not to blow up. "How did he get out then?"

"I don't know," Carter said. "When I woke up this morning, the board and the books were still there. But Carter Junior wasn't."

Nick tried to think. "Was there another opening in the aquarium?"

Carter shook his head. "Nothing. I left a crack at

the top for air. But it was so tiny a grasshopper couldn't have squeezed through."

"Go back to your house and look again," Nick said. "Maybe he's just hiding. I'll call Angelo and we'll meet you there."

"But . . . ," Carter said, clearly not wanting Angelo to know what he'd done. He hung his head. "I guess we need all the help we can get." Ten minutes later, Nick skidded to a stop in front of Carter's house. Angelo's bike was already parked out front. Inside, Carter's four sisters were fighting over the bathroom, while his little brother was glued to cartoons. Nick found Carter and Angelo poking around under Carter's bed and inside his closet. "Find anything?" he asked.

Carter shook his head miserably. He glared at Angelo. "This is your fault. Until I locked him up, Carter Junior never even considered leaving. You scared him off."

Angelo polished his glasses furiously on the front of his shirt. "You have no way of knowing what it was thinking."

"Well, I know now," Carter said. "He hated me closing him in that glass prison and he left."

"Come on, guys," Nick said. "This isn't helping."

103

He examined the aquarium. It was just as Carter had described. The crack was big enough to let in air and no more. "How could he have escaped without moving the books?"

Angelo knelt beside the aquarium. "Perhaps the homunculus has abilities we don't know about yet."

"Maybe he can stretch himself like Plastic Man," Carter said. "That would be awesome."

Nick glanced around, searching for clues. But as chaotic as the room always looked, there was no way to tell if anything was out of place. "Could your brother or one of your sisters have taken it?"

"They never come in here," Carter said. "It's too disgusting for them." Nick could definitely understand that.

"However, if the homunculus got out of the aquarium, it should still be in the house somewhere," Angelo said. "I might have been mistaken about locking it up. But why would it leave its source of food and safety?"

Carter stomped across the room until he was inches away from Angelo. "Carter Junior is not an *it*. He might be little, but he's a person."

Angelo bit his lip. "I know a homunculus looks human. But he's—*it's*—not. It's a creature. A wild

104

creature. Assuming it has human emotions is a mistake."

Nick hated seeing his friends fight. He studied the room and something caught his eye. "Was your window open when you went to bed last night?"

"No." Carter walked over to look. "It was closed last night. I'm sure of it." But it was open several inches now.

Angelo ran his finger across a light spray of dirt on the sill. "Isn't that your screen in the bushes?"

Nick pushed up on the window. It slid all the way open easily. Outside, the dirt beside the rosebush appeared disturbed.

"Come on," he said.

All three boys ran into the yard and looked around. "Where could he have gone?" Carter said. He cupped his hands to his mouth. "Carter Junior! Here, Carter Junior!"

"Are you crazy?" Nick cried. "Do you want all the neighbors to come out and see what we're doing?"

"We have to do something," Carter said. "Maybe we can put up signs. You know, like when you lose your dog."

"Oh, yeah." Nick smirked. "I can just see it. 'Missing:

105

Six-Inch Mythical Creature. Can look and sound like anyone. Loves candy. If you see a miniature version of yourself or someone you know, call 1-800-I-AM-NUTS.'"

Carter kicked a patch of grass. "You have a better plan?"

"Actually," Angelo said, "the candy part isn't a bad idea. Do you have any on you, Carter?"

"Do you even need to ask?" Carter scoffed. He fished through his pockets. "Do you want chocolate, sour, hard, chewy?"

"These should work," Angelo said, taking a package of Skittles from Carter. He ripped open the top and poured several into each of their hands. "The homunculus originally discovered the candy in the closed car, so we have to assume it has an excellent sense of smell. Let's spread out and take these anywhere a small creature might hide—bushes, boxes, enclosed spaces. Maybe we can flush it out with what it likes."

Nick had to admit it was a great plan. But after thirty minutes of searching every yard within a dozen houses—and Carter getting his pants torn by the Murphys' poodle—they hadn't found a single sign of Carter Junior. By then, it was time to leave for school.

"I'm not going to school," Carter said, his jaw locked forward. "Not until I know Carter Junior is safe."

Nick patted him on the back. "I know you're worried. And I promise we won't give up until we get him back. But you can't miss another day of school. Your mom and dad would ground you forever, and then you'd never find him."

"We'll leave the window open and put some candy on the sill," Angelo said. "It's entirely possible that by the time we get out of school he'll be back in your room waiting for you."

Nick knew Angelo was right. But as they slid their bikes into the rack at the back of the school, he couldn't help thinking there were too many pieces that didn't add up. How did the homunculus get out of the aquarium in the first place? And once he did, why leave? There was something else that bothered him too; he just couldn't put his finger on it.

It wasn't until he got up from locking his bike and brushed the dirt off his pants that he realized what they'd missed. "What if Carter Junior didn't escape by himself?"

"What are you thinking?" Angelo asked.

"The dirt on the windowsill. It couldn't have gotten

there from the homunculus climbing *out*."

Angelo rubbed his chin thoughtfully. "But it could have been left by someone opening the window and climbing in from the outside."

"You think someone stole Carter Junior?" Carter said. He rubbed his fist in his palm. "Just tell me who took him and I'll take care of the rest."

Who would have done a thing like that? Almost nobody knew about the homunculus. And of the few people who did, who would have a reason for taking it?

At that moment, three girls came walking across the playground. One was tall and athletic with blond hair. The second was shorter, with dark hair and designer sunglasses. But it was the third—the short one with red hair and a perpetual know-it-all expression on her face—that he focused on. The one person who had both the motive and the opportunity to take the homunculus.

"Angie."

"Hold on," Angelo said as Nick started toward the three girls. "Let's calm down and think this over."

"What's to think about?" Carter snapped. "Angie took Carter Junior and we're getting him back."

"We don't know for sure that anyone took the

homunculus. And even if someone did, we don't know it was Angie."

For someone so smart, Angelo could be totally dense at times. "The clues are all there," Nick said. He held up his fingers, counting the facts. "One, the dirt on the windowsill proves someone climbed inside. Two, Angie's one of the only people who know we have Carter Junior. Three, she just said yesterday that she didn't think taking him back to the woods was a good idea. Four, she lives less than a block from Carter's house. And five . . ." He glared at the smug little face that was always butting into his business. ". . . it's exactly the kind of thing she'd do."

Angelo ran to keep up with him. "We don't know the dirt was tracked in last night. Carter has snuck in and out of his window plenty of times. And he never cleans his room. After yesterday, we have no idea who might have heard about the homunculus. And half the kids in our school live within a block or two of Carter's house."

But Nick was through listening. He raced up to Angie and stopped directly in front of her. "Give him back."

Angie blinked. "Excuse me?"

Carter flexed his skinny arms and cracked his knuckles. "We know you stole Carter Junior."

Dana put a hand to her mouth. "Someone took the homunculus?"

"Not *someone*," Nick said, glaring at Angie. "You."

"We don't know that for a fact," Angelo said. "You're jumping to conclusions based largely on assumptions and limited data."

"She said yesterday that she thought we should let scientists study him and put him in a zoo," Nick said.

Angie glared back at Nick. "I'm not the one who said that. Dana is. And she wasn't suggesting you put him in a zoo. Just that it might be valuable to learn more about a new species."

"Who cares?" Carter said. "Just give him back or there's going to be trouble."

Tiffany gave Carter a nasty grin. "I could handle you with both arms in a cast. And which one of you wants to fight Dana?"

"No one's fighting anyone," Angie said. "If your homunculus has escaped, we'll help you get him back."

"We could use the extra eyes," Angelo said.

"We don't need their help," Nick muttered.

"Are you sure about that?" Angelo asked. "We didn't do so well on our own."

Nick scuffed his shoe across the playground gravel. He still didn't trust Angie. But by keeping her and her friends around, it would make it that much easier to find out if they had taken the homunculus. Besides, Angelo was right. If Carter Junior had run off, they could use all the help they could get in finding him. He nodded. "Okay, fine. But you girls better not get in the way."

CHAPTER 13

I LOVE A TASTY HOT DOG WITH MUSTARD, ONIONS, A SHARP DILL PICKLE, AND JUST A HINT OF CELERY SALT. KEEP READING. I'LL BE RIGHT BACK

All through school that morning, Nick tried to think of a plan to prove Angie's guilt or innocence. The best he could come up with was a lie detector test, but although he had full confidence Angelo could build one, that would be a waste of valuable searching time. Besides, he didn't know if Angie would even agree to take the test. And if she did, she could probably beat it. She seemed like the kind of person who would be a good liar.

Ms. Schoepf didn't make concentrating easy. Everyone except Angelo and Dana had flunked the math test. So the class spent all morning studying how to solve for Y in mixed equations. After an hour of "If X equals 7/4 and Y is equal to the sum of 6x + 6/x," Nick thought that if he never saw another fraction in his life it would be too soon.

As if that wasn't enough, Kimber Tidwell apparently didn't feel like she was getting enough attention. Thirty minutes into the math lesson, she complained of a sick stomach and asked to visit the nurse. Nick was pretty sure what she was actually sick of was variables, and he wished he'd thought of going to the nurse first.

But then, fifteen minutes after leaving, she walked back into class.

"Feeling better?" Ms. Schoepf asked.

"Much." Kimber smiled. "I think I was just sick of hats." She pulled off a green knitted cap that looked like something a dill pickle might put on its ugly baby and stuffed it into her coat pocket.

"Interesting as that may be," Ms. Schoepf said, "let's save the fashion discussion for outside class and get back to our math."

"Or we could talk about both," Tiffany whispered under her breath. "Kimber's taste in clothes times any number always equals zero."

Ms. Schoepf gave Tiffany a warning look. "Kimber, please take your seat so we can go over reducing fractions."

Kimber's lip pooched out. "Do we have to? Isn't there something a little less boring we could talk about?" She turned to Rebel and Torrie. "You, for example. Why is it that the two of you always do everything I tell you? Like wearing those stupid hats. Don't either of you have the guts to stand up to me and admit how ridiculous they look?"

Rebel and Torrie stared at Kimber. Rebel reached for her hat as if unsure whether she should take it off or leave it on.

"Kimber Tidwell!" Ms. Schoepf said. "Take your seat at once or you'll be talking to the principal."

"An excellent idea," Kimber said. "It's about time someone explained that her frumpy shoes went out of style when we were all wearing diapers. Designer diapers for me, of course." With that, she twirled around and flounced out of class.

Carter leaned over to Nick. "I think all those hats must have been starving her brain of oxygen."

Ms. Schoepf stared at the door, obviously bewildered by Kimber's performance, before turning back to the class. "Everyone, just . . . read your history books."

When Kimber hadn't returned by lunch, Torrie and Rebel wandered around the cafeteria, looking unsure without their leader. Finally they each took off their

hats and ate by themselves.

By the end of the day, rumors were flying around school. Kimber had been suspended. She'd had a nervous breakdown. She'd been taken from the school in an ambulance.

"She just wants attention," Tiffany said. "Trust me, she'll wait until everyone's outside to make her grand reappearance."

Sure enough, just after the final bell, a pale-looking Kimber strode onto the playground. Nick noticed she was once again wearing her puke-green hat. Seeing everyone watching her, she threw back her head and flipped her skirt. "Nurse thinks I might have had a touch of food poisoning. I'm never eating non–organically grown artichokes again."

"More like a touch of brain poisoning," Carter said, making Tiffany laugh.

Kimber shot a laser-beam glare at him before making a beeline for Rebel and Torrie. Nick didn't think either of them looked especially excited to see her. He couldn't blame them. He'd rather have no friends at all than friends like that—even if she was the most popular girl in school.

As the three of them gathered together, Nick could just overhear Kimber say, "Why aren't you wearing

115

your hats? Do you want to end up with early wrinkles and age spots? Not to mention the ever-present threat of skin cancer?"

Within seconds, the group was surrounded by kids asking Kimber how she was feeling. Nick shook his head, wondering what people saw in her. When he turned back to his own friends, Angelo, Carter, and the girls were staring at him.

"Well?" Angie asked.

He realized he must have missed something. "Sorry, what did you say?"

"You might have heard if you weren't all googly-eyed over Kimber."

"I wasn't googly-eyed," he muttered. "I was just wondering what her deal was."

"Her deal is that she needs to be the center of attention everywhere she goes," Tiffany said.

"We were asking you what the plan is," Dana said. "How should we go about finding the homunculus?"

Nick wasn't sure how he'd been elected captain of the Carter Junior search team. "Well, first we should probably go to Carter's house and see if he's come back. If not, he likes candy and Mountain Dew. I guess we should spread out and try to lure him in with those."

"We'll go get our bikes and meet you there," Angie said.

"You really don't think they had anything to do with his disappearance?" Nick asked as he pulled his bike out of the rack.

"Why would they offer to help us if they did?" Angelo asked.

"To make us think they're innocent," Carter said. "I saw something just like it on TV once. The kidnappers join in the search so they can find out how much the authorities really know. What we have to do is blow their cover by asking trick questions. Things they wouldn't know unless they actually had him. Then, *pow!* We slam the net on them."

"There are no authorities," Angelo said, stopping to wait for the light to turn green so they could cross the street. "And think about it. If Angie and her friends have the homunculus, the last thing they'd want to do is hang around with us. Remember how hard it was to keep people from discovering him?"

"Hopefully he'll be at your house when we get back," Nick said.

Carter nodded. "I'm crossing my fingers and toes. If I thought I could ride home with my eyes crossed, I'd do that too."

Unfortunately, nothing had changed when they reached his house. The window was still open, the candy was still on the sill, and his room was still empty.

As soon as Angie, Dana, and Tiffany showed up, the six of them scoured the neighborhood. Using a city map Dana had printed out and a check sheet Angelo had made, they covered every house, yard, and vacant lot for two blocks in all directions. But there was no sign of the homunculus anywhere. No cookie trail. No tiny footprints. No familiar voices. Nothing.

By then it was nearly dark and they had to admit it was time to give up for the day. Everyone was dirty and exhausted. Carter looked like he was fighting not to cry.

"Let's ride down to Caspers and I'll treat you all to a hot dog," Angie said. When Nick gave her a questioning look, she gave a half smile and said, "I've been doing a lot of babysitting lately. I'm nearly as rich as Kimber's family."

Caspers was the best hot dog place in the world. According to Nick's dad it was more than fifty years old, and he had eaten there when he was a boy. All of them ordered regular hot dogs and sodas, except for Carter, who ordered a chili cheese dog with extra chili, cheese, and onions—which earned him a "That-a-boy"

from the grandmotherly woman who served them.

"It's like he floated into thin air," Nick said, taking a bite of his hot dog.

Angie rattled the ice of her Coke. "Maybe he *can* fly and we just don't know it."

Angelo rubbed his sweaty face, smearing mustard across his cheek. "Not unless it has wings we haven't seen."

"Have you ever considered that the homunculus might be able to change into things other than humans?" Dana asked. "For all we know it turned into a bird and that's why it didn't leave any tracks." She pointed to Angelo's cheek and he quickly wiped his face with a napkin.

Angelo flipped open his notebook. "If it can, it's something other than a homunculus. There's not much information out there. But one thing everyone seems to agree on is that homunculi are small, beardless humans."

Carter crammed half his hot dog and a huge spoonful of chili into his mouth—chewing it all with a loud *smack-smack-smack*.

"Disgusting," Tiffany said, turning away.

"Hey, I eat when I'm depressed," Carter said, wolfing down another big spoonful of chili.

Nick grinned. "And happy, tired, confused, excited, and bored. Not to mention hungry."

Angie toyed with the dill pickle spear on her hot dog before looking at each of them. "I know this isn't what you want to hear. But I think we need to at least consider the possibility that the reason we haven't found the homunculus may be the most obvious."

"What's that?" Nick asked.

"Because he went home. And if that's the case, we'll never know for sure."

CHAPTER 14

IF I EVER START A ROCK BAND, I WILL DEFINITELY NAME IT BENJAMIN'S MOLARS

The six kids rode home silently, each splitting off toward their homes until only Nick and Carter were left. As they coasted to a stop in front of Nick's house, Nick punched Carter lightly on the shoulder. "Don't give up, buddy. Who knows? You might wake up tomorrow and there he'll be, sitting on your bed eating a candy bar."

Carter kicked his bike pedal with the toe of one sneaker, making it spin. "I don't know. I think Angie might be right. I don't think we'll ever know what happened to him for sure. I just hope he didn't . . . you know . . . get eaten by a dog or a cat or something."

"Hey, this is Carter Junior we're talking about,"

Nick said. "Do you really think your namesake could be stopped by something as ordinary as a cat?"

Carter sniffed. "Probably not. I'll bet Carter Junior could handle a mountain lion. After all, he lived in the woods."

"Right." Nick watched his friend ride off before wheeling his bike up the driveway. As he walked into the house, Mom was standing in front of the stove. Nick sniffed the air. Despite the fact that he'd eaten less than an hour before, his stomach rumbled at the enticing aroma. "Something smells good."

"Chicken Marsala," Mom said. "It's your dad's favorite."

Nick frowned. "He's still bummed out about the camping trip?"

"Yes. But don't worry. It's just a temporary funk. He'll get over it in no time."

Upstairs a door closed and footsteps sounded on the stairs. "Don't say I told you anything," Mom said. "Act normal."

"Sure." Nicked dropped into a chair and quickly opened one of his textbooks. But if his dad was still depressed about the camping trip, he didn't show it. He walked up to Nick with a big grin on his face and ruffled his hair.

"Hello, son. Pounding the books, huh?"

Nick glanced at his mom, who gave him an encouraging smile. "Um, yeah. Just catching up on my math."

"Good thing." Dad grinned. "You're going to need it when you hear the news. I've decided it's time to increase your allowance. I think doubling it seems about right. How does that sound to you?"

"Sounds great!" Nick said. If this was a funk, his dad could be in one all the time.

"Double?" Mom asked. "Are you sure that isn't a little much?"

"Nothing is too much for my family," Dad said, a huge grin plastered across his face.

Nick didn't think he'd ever seen his father this happy. It was a little creepy.

"Speaking of family," Dad said, walking to Mom. "What are you doing slaving over a hot stove on a wonderful night like tonight?"

Mom gave Dad the kind of uncertain smile you might give a recently released mental patient. "I'm . . . cooking."

"Nonsense!" Dad pulled her away from the stove and spun her around. "Didn't I tell you I'm taking us all out for dinner? I'm thinking that new Italian place that opened up last week."

Mom's mouth dropped open, but she didn't say a

word. Nick didn't think he'd ever seen her look so flabbergasted.

"Wait right here," Dad said. "I just need to grab my keys and put on some cologne." Before Mom could respond, he turned and raced up the stairs.

Nick looked at his mother. "Okay, that is just about the weirdest thing I've ever seen."

Mom raised a hand as if she was going to say something, then lowered it and shook her head. Slowly she turned off the stove. "Grab your coat. I guess we're going out."

Nick got up from the table, walked to his room, and put on his coat. He was glad his dad was feeling better. And an increase in his allowance would be great. But there was something so strange about the way his dad had been acting.

Mom was just putting the chicken in the refrigerator when Dad came back into the kitchen. "You know," she said with a smile, "it's probably a good idea to go out to dinner. It's been a while since we went to a nice restaurant."

As Mom shut the refrigerator door, Dad walked into the kitchen and looked at Nick, who was zipping up his coat. "Where are you going?"

124

"Out to dinner?" Nick said. His father's former good cheer was gone, replaced by a slightly perturbed expression.

"Oh," Dad said. "Going with friends?"

Nick had no idea how to respond to that. But his dad didn't seem to notice. He rubbed his forehead.

"Are you feeling all right?" Mom asked. "You look a little pale."

"I'm fine." Dad looked at the stove. "What's for dinner? Didn't I smell something cooking?"

Mom tilted her head. "I thought we were going out."

Dad threw his hands in the air. "Why am I the last one to hear these things?" He sighed and turned to go back up the stairs. "Let me get my keys. I sure hope we're not going anywhere fancy. The last thing I want to do is dress up and put on cologne."

Nick looked at his mom. "Is he losing it?"

She pressed her lips together. "He's been under a lot of stress."

Nick guessed that was true. But he also had a feeling he might not be getting his allowance increase.

The next morning, things seemed to be more or less back to normal. Nick's dad wasn't manically happy or

125

inexplicably depressed. Carter Junior still hadn't turned up, but Nick was starting to think that might be for the best.

"It would have been tough smuggling him up to the mountains on a bus without our parents finding out. He's probably somewhere in the woods right now," Nick said as the boys rode their bikes to school, "hanging out with his homunculus buddies, drinking Mountain Dew they stole from people camping nearby, and doing amazing celebrity impressions."

Carter smiled sadly. "I guess. I just miss him reading comic books with me and eating my candy."

Angelo skidded his bike to a halt, and Nick had to make a sharp left turn to keep from running into him. "Is that Old Man Dashner?"

"Huh?" Nick turned to see a gray-haired man jogging down the street. Runners weren't unusual in Pleasant Hill. Every morning the boys passed five or six joggers on their way to school. But as far as he could remember, Old Man Dashner had never been one of them. In fact, the only time Nick ever saw Mr. Dashner leave his house was when he got the mail or chased off kids crossing his lawn. But the jogging wasn't even the weirdest part.

Carter burst into surprised laughter. "What's he wearing?"

For as long as Nick had known him, Old Man Dashner's clothing had consisted of khaki pants pulled up halfway to his chest, faded plaid shirts buttoned to the neck, and floppy brown slippers. His idea of a fashion statement was putting on a corduroy jacket when it got cold.

But now he was running down the middle of the street in what looked like a pink one-piece women's swimsuit, plaid golf pants rolled up at the ankles, and a Viking helmet, complete with horns.

"Hello, boys!" Dashner shouted as he trotted past. "Nothing like a morning run to get the old ticker in *tick-tock* shape."

"Did he just make a joke?" Carter asked.

"Did he actually talk to us without using the words *trespassing*, *police*, or *nuisance*?" Nick said.

Angelo reached for his monster notebook, then seemed to change his mind. "It has to be some kind of episode. Maybe we should call the police to get him some help."

"Not me," Carter said, pedaling his bike away. "Dashner already hates me enough for that time I

accidentally knocked out his mailbox with my electric scooter."

Nick scratched his head. "Maybe it's some kind of really, really late midlife crisis. If I was stuck in that house all by myself, I'd probably go Froot Loops too." He shook his head and watched the old man jog away. "It doesn't get any weirder than that."

After the excitement of the last few days, it was a relief when the boys got to school and discovered Ms. Schoepf was out sick, leaving them with a substitute teacher.

"Maybe she's one of those subs who'll let us watch movies all day," Carter said.

Angelo pulled his books out of his backpack. "What would be the point of that? We can watch movies at home. School is for learning."

Carter patted him sadly on the shoulder. "Sometimes I wonder why we are even friends. I can only assume it's so I can keep you from withering away into nothing but a giant brain."

Nick didn't care one way or the other, as long as they didn't spend another day solving for x, y, and z and trying to change upside-down fractions into integers.

But just before the bell rang, Ms. Schoepf came bustling through the door, her arms loaded down with a large black case and several bags. "Sorry I'm late."

The substitute, a tall, bony woman with frizzy hair, got up from behind Ms. Schoepf's desk. "I thought you were out sick."

"I was," Ms. Schoepf said. "But I'm feeling fine now."

Carter leaned over to Nick and whispered, "What's that she's carrying?"

Nick studied the black case. It looked sort of like a guitar. But as far as he knew, Ms. Schoepf didn't play any instruments. In fact, she'd once mentioned wishing that she'd been born with even an ounce of musical talent.

The substitute teacher looked flustered. She straightened her glasses and tugged at her skirt. "I drove all the way across town to get here. Who's going to pay me for my time?"

"Talk to the principal," Ms. Schoepf said. "I'm sure she'll work it all out. It's really none of my concern."

Nick felt bad for the woman as she gathered up her things and left. It wasn't like Ms. Schoepf to be so rude. Especially to someone who'd been doing her a favor by filling in.

As soon as the sub was out the door, Ms. Schoepf whipped open the black case. It *was* a guitar. "Boys and girls," she said, sitting on her desk and resting the guitar on her lap, "why do you think you've been struggling so much with math?"

Angelo raised his hand. "Because people haven't been doing their homework?"

"I did my homework," said a boy with red hair. "I do my homework every day."

"Whatever," Nick muttered. Rob Wells was the biggest liar in sixth grade and everyone knew it. Nick raised his hand. "I think it's the variables. If we could just stick with numbers and leave out the letters, it would be a lot easier."

"All good answers," Ms. Schoepf said. "But I've given it a great deal of thought, and I've decided that math would be much more interesting if we put it to music."

"You mean like scales and time signatures?" Dana asked. "Math and music have a lot more in common than many people realize."

"Actually," Ms. Schoepf said, "I was thinking more of the driving beat of hard rock, with the mind-numbing chords of acoustic guitar." She shook back her head,

ran her fingers through her hair, strummed a series of chords that didn't go together, and burst into singing that could best be described as excruciating.

Compound fractions are a total pain.
I can't find all the values in the right domain.
A coefficient matrix sets my heart on fire.
But a common logarithm sends me higher, higher,
  higher!
Domain, double root, conjugated pair.
Complex number formulas, I see them everywhere.

Sitting in their desks, the kids stared in shock and a little bit of horror. Nick didn't think he'd ever heard anything so terrible in his life. Not only could Ms. Schoepf not play at all, but Nick didn't think the guitar was even in tune.

Angie put her hands over her ears. "Is this some kind of joke?"

"I once heard a cat get its head get stuck in a rain gutter," Carter said, raising his voice to be heard over the teacher's screaming. "It sounded much better than this."

Kimber Tidwell raised her hand and shouted, "Can

131

I go to the nurse again?"

"Button it up, Buttercup!" Ms. Schoepf yelled, still strumming wildly. "I've got six more verses."

The rest of the day didn't get any better. During history, Ms. Schoepf did an interpretive dance that she claimed paid homage to Abraham Lincoln's hair and the woman who sold Benjamin Franklin his false teeth. In science, she nearly lit the curtains on fire with what she called "a display of totally awesome pyrotechnics that will make heavy metal concerts look like tea parties." And in English she asked the entire class to write an essay on what the world would look like if we all had zucchini slices for eyes.

By the time they finally stumbled out of class at the end of the day, the kids all felt like they'd been through a war zone.

"I am *not* going back to that class," Kimber sobbed.

"I'm telling my mom," Rebel said. "Ms. Schoepf has gone completely crazy."

"I kind of liked the interpretive dance," Carter said. He waved his arms and warbled the words Ms. Schoepf had been repeating. "Abraham Lincoln with his head full of rollers. Thank you for the woman who gave Benjamin his molars."

Nick didn't know what to think. That morning he'd

been sure nothing could be weirder than Old Man Dashner's outfit. But after Ms. Schoepf, Mr. Dashner looked totally normal. It was like the whole city was going crazy.

CHAPTER 15

I MUST ADMIT, IF SOMEONE STUCK GUM TO MY AUTOMOBILE, I WOULD BE RATHER IRATE AS WELL

On the way home, the boys tried to remember if they'd ever had a more bizarre day.

"There was that time in second grade when Carter stuck a peanut in his ear and couldn't get it out," Nick said. "I still remember how hard everyone laughed when you told the teacher why you had to go to the nurse."

Carter huffed. "What? Rob Wells told me that if you didn't wash the dirt out of your ears you could grow plants in them. I thought it would be totally cool to have peanuts anytime you wanted. Besides, it was a lot weirder when *you* turned into a zombie," Carter said.

"Sure," Nick agreed. "But at least that made sense when we figured it all out. Today was just totally random."

"Or was it?" Angelo pulled his bike to the side of the road.

Nick skidded to a stop beside him. "What do you mean?"

"I'm not sure. It's just . . ." Angelo bent over and wrapped his arms around his chest.

"Are you okay?" Nick asked. Angelo looked a little pale, the way Kimber had after coming back from the nurse.

Angelo breathed heavily for a minute or two before nodding. "I felt a little dizzy for a minute, but I'm okay now." He got back on his bike and started pedaling. "Let's check on Mr. Dashner to make sure he's all right."

"Are you kidding?" Carter squealed. "Let's just check the dental work on a great white shark while we're at it. Or offer to let Chuck Norris try out his latest karate moves on us."

"He's got a point," Nick said. "I mean, Old Man Dashner's never been exactly thrilled to see us."

Angelo pedaled faster, and Carter, who had the shortest legs of the three and the oldest bike, barely kept up despite pedaling nearly twice as fast as the other two. "He threatened to feed me to his pet piranhas if I ever came within fifty feet of his house again. All because I accidentally got stuck to the back window of his car. Well, that and the mailbox thing."

"Which makes it twice as strange that he was so friendly this morning," Angelo said. "You two can do what you want, but I'm going to check on him. Something isn't adding up." He turned his bike into Mr. Dashner's driveway.

"We better cover his back," Nick said. He followed Angelo, even though he thought he'd rather approach a sleeping bear in its cave than Mr. Dashner in his house.

Carter looked toward the sky and said, "God, if I get killed, make it quick and painless. And make it not by piranha, or crossbow, or acid or—"

"Are you coming or not?" Nick asked.

"Amen," Carter said, hurrying after him.

"Since when are you religious?" Nick asked as they got off their bikes.

Carter wiped the sweat off his forehead and grinned nervously. "Since I realized we are going to see the devil."

Old Man Dashner watched his yard like an eagle. If

136

a kid looked like he was even thinking about stepping onto the lawn, Dashner was outside shouting threats. So Nick was surprised that they got almost all the way to the door before the door flew open.

"Who's out there? What do you want? Is it the milk-man?" At least he was back in his khakis and plaid shirt. Nick wasn't sure he could deal with a cranky old man in a pink swimsuit.

Angelo glanced back toward Nick with a quizzical look. Nick stepped back, ready to take off at a moment's notice, but Angelo kept walking. "We just wanted to check on you."

"Check on me?" Mr. Dashner barked. He ran his fingers through his wild gray hair with a confused sort of expression. "What do you mean, *check on me*? More likely coming to throw eggs at my door. Don't think I didn't hear you sneaking through my yard the night before last either."

Angelo paused a few feet short of the front steps. Nick didn't blame him. He'd heard that the old man carried a cane with a razor-sharp blade that popped out of the end. The last thing he'd want to do was get within swinging distance. "We're not going to throw any eggs. It's just that when we saw you jogging this morning,"

Angelo said, "you didn't seem like yourself."

"Jogging?" Mr. Dashner spat. "Do I look like one of them crazy fools who sweat in public for enjoyment? Listen here, I've been a little under the weather today, but I can still deal with a handful of trouble-making scoundrels." He leaned a little farther out, and the dazed look in his eyes disappeared as he spotted Carter. "You!" he shouted, poking a knobby finger in Carter's direction. "You're the brat who stuck gum to the back of my car!"

Carter backed toward his bike. "You, uh, must be thinking of some other kid."

Old Man Dashner rubbed his eyes and squinted. "It's you all right. Didn't I tell you I'd feed you to my piranhas if I saw you again?"

The old man started down the steps and Carter made a break for it. "I'm out of here," he screamed, jumping on his bike and pedaling furiously.

Nick grabbed the back of Angelo's shirt. "Time to go."

"I just wanted to ask you about this morning," Angelo said. "Did you feel unusual in any way?"

"I'll make you feel unusual." Old Man Dashner grabbed a stick from beside his steps, brandishing it like

a sword. "Teach you young troublemakers to bother peaceful folks."

Nick yanked on Angelo—who finally seemed to realize talking was no longer an option—and the two of them grabbed their bikes and ran down the driveway.

"That's right, you run!" Mr. Dashner shouted, waving his stick. "And keep running too! Next time, I'm calling the cops."

"Didn't I tell you he was crazy?" Carter said when Nick and Angelo had caught up with him.

Angelo shook his head. "Cranky, yes. And possibly violent. But not crazy."

Nick panted, trying to catch his breath. "If there's a difference, I'm not seeing it."

"This morning was crazy. What we saw back there was just angry."

Carter laughed. "Dude, that's exactly my point. This morning he's running around in a pink swimsuit. This afternoon he's waving sticks and threatening to feed me to the fish version of a food processor. That's crazy, cuckoo, nuts, mixed up in the melon."

Angelo tapped the picture. "Except that I'm almost positive the person who just threatened us on his porch has no memory of being this person. And did you hear

139

him ask if I was the *milkman*? There hasn't been milk delivery in Pleasant Hill since before we were born."

"What are you saying?" Nick asked. "You think he has that thing where older people can't remember stuff? What's it called, all timers?"

"Alzheimer's," Angelo said. "A form of dementia most common in people sixty-five and older. The most common symptom is forgetfulness, which could explain why he doesn't remember that he was out jogging in a Viking helmet this morning. And yet he not only recognized Carter, he also remembered that Carter put gum on his car, and that he threatened to feed him to a species of fish illegal in the U.S."

Nick hadn't thought of that. "But if he can remember all that, why can't he remember what he did this morning?"

"It's my curse," Carter said. "People remember things I did that even *I've* forgotten about."

"I don't know." Angelo pulled his pen out of his monster notebook book and chewed on the back. "Don't you think it's quite a coincidence that Mr. Dashner decides to dress up and go running on the same day that Ms. Schoepf freaks out?"

"You think she has old-timers too?" Carter asked

140

with a grin. "Maybe she'll forget I didn't turn in my English assignment last week."

"It's Alzheimer's, not old-timers," Angelo said. "And I don't think Ms. Schoepf or Old Man Dashner has it. Something weird is happening around here. And I want to figure out what. Come on, let's head back to my house."

As the three of them neared Angelo's house, Nick noticed Angie, Dana, and Tiffany standing in the front yard. "What are they doing here?" he asked.

"Maybe they found Carter Junior," Carter said, racing ahead.

When Nick and Angelo got there, Angie was folding her arms with an annoyed expression on her face. "It took you long enough."

"Long enough for what?" Nick asked.

Carter tossed his bike on the grass. "Did you find Carter Junior?"

Tiffany looked up from texting on her pink, rhinestone-covered phone. "How could we when we've been waiting here for you? It's rude to tell someone to hurry to your house and then not be there when you said."

Angelo opened the calendar on his iPad. "Did we have an appointment?"

Angie gritted her teeth. "Is this your idea of a joke? Because I'm not in the mood for it. First you're all, 'I know everything. I'm so smart. Meet me at my house.' Then you don't even show up."

Nick held up his hands. "Whoa, whoa, whoa, back up. Who told you to meet us here?"

Dana slammed a basketball on the concrete driveway and caught it in a graceful swipe of one hand. "Come on, guys. This isn't funny. I'm missing basketball practice. Angelo, you said it was really important that we meet you as soon as possible—and you were kind of snotty about it. I thought you'd found the homunculus. Now, do you or do you not have something to tell us?"

Angelo wiped his glasses on his shirt, with the same thoughtful look he'd had earlier. "When exactly did I tell you to meet me here?"

Dana rolled the ball from hand to hand with an uncertain expression. "Right after school."

"He couldn't have," Nick said. "He's been with us the whole time. We were checking up on Old Man Dashner to see why he was jogging in a women's bathing suit."

Angie's cheeks flamed bright red. "You guys are jerks. See if we ever help you again." She spun around and stomped away. "Let's go."

Dana shook her head and gave Angelo a disappointed frown. Tiffany followed Angie, still typing on her phone. "Trust me," she said. "The Twitterverse is going to know you guys are losers with a capital L. Hashtag peabrain."

"What was that all about?" Carter asked. "This day just keeps getting weirder and weirder. First Dashner, then Ms. Schoepf, and now Angie, Dana, and Tiffany. It's like the whole world is catching the crazy disease."

"That's exactly what it's like," Angelo said. He grabbed Carter by the elbow. "For once I think you've hit the atom directly in the nucleus."

Carter wrinkled his nose. "Say what?"

Angelo opened his notebook, writing and talking at the same time. "One of those things by themselves might be a coincidence. Old Man Dashner might have had a crazy urge to go running. Ms. Schoepf might have adopted a radical new teaching style. And Angie . . . well, maybe she was just messing with us. But taken all together, it can't be a coincidence."

Nick suddenly remembered something else. "My dad started acting really strange last night. One minute he was all happy, giving me a raise in my allowance and promising to take us out to dinner. But two minutes

143

later, it was like it never happened."

Angelo wrote so fast his hand was almost a blur. "There is something going on here. Something big. I don't know what it is. But I know someone who might." He grabbed his bike. "Let's go to the library."

CHAPTER 16

WAS THE ENTRANCE TOO DRAMATIC? REALLY, YOU CAN TELL ME

The Pleasant Hill library was a one-story glass-and-brick building. It didn't look that big from the outside. And even inside it appeared to be like any other library—a checkout desk, children's section, fiction and nonfiction shelves. But in the far back, behind the reference desk, was an area few people ever saw. Nick hadn't even known about it until Angelo took him there shortly after an amulet had turned Nick into a zombie.

If it hadn't been for the help of an unusual man, Nick might have remained a zombie forever. It wasn't the only time the man had gotten the boys out of a jam either. He'd saved their bacon again at a school called Sumina Prep, which ended up being the laboratory of a mad scientist. He called himself a reference librarian, but Nick had an idea he was much more than that.

"Is Mr. Blackham in?" Angelo asked the gray-haired woman sorting books at the reference desk.

She looked up and smiled sweetly. "Oh, it's you three again. Did your girlfriends come with you?"

Nick felt his cheeks burn. The last time they'd come looking for Mr. Blackham, it was with Angie, Dana, and Tiffany. But the woman clucked her tongue. "Not girlfriend like the kids say now, dear. But a girl who is your friend. That's what it meant in my day, you know."

Nick shrugged. "Um, no. They didn't come."

"Well, that's just fine. I believe Mr. Blackham is doing some kind of investigation in the back. He's been in there all day poring over dusty old books." She wrinkled her nose and jingled her silver bracelets. "I keep telling him he needs to read Percy Jackson or maybe Harry Potter. Something exciting like that. But he's had his nose stuck in German folklore all day."

"*German*?" Angelo said. He gave a meaningful look to Nick and Carter. "We'll go look for him."

"You do that," the woman said. As the boys walked by, she chuckled. "Oh, and I'm glad everything worked out with that nasty business up at Sumina Prep."

Nick turned around. How did she know about

Sumina? "Do you think she knows things too, like Mr. Blackham?" he whispered.

"Nah," Carter said. "He probably just tells her stuff."

In the back of the library there were no windows to let in sunlight that might damage the valuable books. What few lights there were buzzed and flickered, casting the room in the dull gray of a cloudy afternoon.

The noises of the main library seemed to fade the farther in they went, and the boys' footsteps sounded louder than they should have. It was almost like another world. A world of tall, looming shelves with thick, dusty books. Nick glanced over his shoulder, wondering how a building this small could seem so big inside.

At last they reached an alcove set into the far back of the building. At the center of the opening stood a large metal desk covered with books, bottles, pieces of what looked like very old pottery, and even a couple of small statues. A nameplate on the front of the desk read BARTHOLOMEW BLACKHAM, REFERENCE LIBRARIAN.

The boys looked around, but the librarian was nowhere in sight. "Mr. Blackham?" Angelo called. Although he spoke softly, his voice seemed loud in the silence of the dim space, and a cloud of dust motes swirled in the air.

"I don't think he's here," Carter whispered.

147

Nick looked longingly toward the bright light of the main library. "Maybe we should—"

A shadow fell over them, cutting off his words. A fluttering sounded from overhead and all three of them looked up.

"Can I help you?" a voice asked from behind them.

Nick turned with a start to find a pale man in a long, black coat standing directly behind him. He had no idea how the librarian had gotten there without him seeing.

"Holy diaper change," Carter muttered. "You scared the you-know-what out of me."

"Mr. Blackham," Angelo said. "We need your help. Something really weird is going on."

The librarian nodded, his piercing eyes studying each of the boys, one by one. At last he set the books he was holding on the desk and took a seat. "Tell me everything."

Angelo told Mr. Blackham about Mr. Dashner and Ms. Schoepf. Carter told him about Angie and her friends thinking they had seen Angelo. Nick finished by telling him what had happened with his father. The librarian didn't take a single note, but Nick got the feeling he hadn't missed a thing.

"Very interesting," Mr. Blackham said, pulling off

his leather gloves. "And you believe these things are related?"

"Don't you?" Nick asked. "I mean, it would be a pretty big coincidence if they randomly happened at the same time."

"Coincidence is the province of rubes and verdant storytellers," the librarian said.

Nick didn't know what that meant. But he thought the librarian was agreeing with him.

"So," Carter said, "do you know what's causing everyone to turn whacko all of a sudden?"

The librarian furrowed his brow in concentration. He ran a hand over one of the thick leather volumes on his desk. Finally he sighed. "No."

"No?" Angelo gasped, looking like he'd just been hit in the head with a board. Nick couldn't blame him. After the last two times the librarian had helped them, he just sort of figured Mr. Blackham knew everything.

"I wish I did," the librarian said. "Something is clearly happening here and I've been doing my best to learn what. But at this point . . . I'm just not sure."

Nick looked at his friends with a sick feeling. If even Mr. Blackham didn't know what was going on, what chance did they have of figuring it out? "Well, if you can't help us, you can't help us."

Angelo squeezed his hands together. "Thanks for trying."

The boys began to turn away, but the librarian stopped them. "Are you familiar with the term *causality*?"

Both Nick and Carter turned to Angelo. Angelo stared at the ceiling, thinking. "Isn't that figuring out why something happens?"

Mr. Blackham clapped his hands silently. "Very good. The Greek philosopher Aristotle defined four chief types of cause. Material, what something is made of. Formal, its form or nature. Efficient, the thing that immediately effected its change. And final, the thing's ultimate goal."

Angelo nodded uncertainly. "So . . ."

"So to solve your problem, you must first determine what started things, as Carter put it, 'turning whacko.'"

Nick was confused. "You're saying to figure out what's causing everyone to start acting weird, we need to figure out what made them *start* acting weird?"

"Precisely." The librarian smiled until he could tell they didn't have a clue what he was talking about. "Think back," he said. "Is there anything that happened just before people in your neighborhood began behaving oddly? Anything out of the ordinary you

150

might have failed to mention?"

Nick got a sick feeling in the pit of his stomach. He looked at Carter.

"Well . . ." Carter shuffled his feet on the thin carpet. "Something did happen. But it couldn't have had anything to do with this."

The librarian waited, his face a study in patience.

It was Angelo who finally broke the silence. "Over the weekend, we found something in the woods."

Mr. Blackham's eyebrows rose ever so slightly. "*Something?*"

Nick felt bad making Angelo take all the blame. "We think it was a homunculus. We were planning on taking it back where it belonged. But the night before last, it disappeared. We've been hoping it went back to where we found it."

"I see." The librarian tapped his fingers on a pair of thick books that were written in a language Nick thought must be German. "And this was how long before people began acting strangely?"

"If you count my dad, the day before."

"It was my fault," Carter blurted. "I took Carter Junior without telling them."

Angelo hung his head. "But I was the one who told him to put it in the aquarium. That's why it ran away."

151

"Do you think that really has something to do with what's going on?" Nick asked. "I don't see how the homunculus escaping could have anything to do with people acting weird."

Mr. Blackham pursed his lips. "It's difficult to say. But at this point it does seem the most likely efficient. Unless you can think of any other recent causality?"

All three boys shook their heads.

"If Carter Junior running away really did cause all this, what can we do about it?" Nick asked. "We've looked for him everywhere."

"And I've read everything I can find on homunculi," Angelo said. "I never saw anything about making people act crazy."

Mr. Blackham stood. "I recommend you think back to everything you've seen. Everything you've noted. Try looking at it from a new perspective. A different angle."

"That's it?" Carter asked. "You're not going to help us make it right?"

Mr. Blackham pulled on his gloves. "This new information will take some looking into. To be perfectly frank, I'm never seen an actual homunculus. I shall begin researching it immediately. In any case, I do not have a shadow of a doubt that you will find a way to

identify the problem and fix it." Without another word, he nodded and disappeared into the rows of shelves.

"You think he's just messing with us?" Carter asked as they walked toward the front of the library.

"Maybe he wants us to figure things out on our own," Nick said. "So we can become true monster hunters."

Angelo shook his head. "I think for once we've come across something he can't solve for us. We're going to *have* to figure this out on our own."

Nick was all for solving his own problems. But he didn't have the first clue where to look. "I don't get the part about looking at things from a different perspective. What are we supposed to be looking at?"

The three boys stepped outside, where the sun was starting to set. Nick checked his watch. It was almost five.

"Let's go to my house," Angelo said. "And start from the beginning."

CHAPTER 17

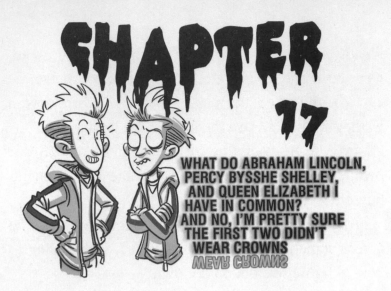

WHAT DO ABRAHAM LINCOLN, PERCY BYSSHE SHELLEY, AND QUEEN ELIZABETH I HAVE IN COMMON? AND NO, I'M PRETTY SURE THE FIRST TWO DIDN'T WEAR CROWNS

"Okay," Angelo said, sitting down at a desk covered with notes and books. "Let's get started."

"What is all this stuff?" Nick asked.

"Research," Angelo said, as if the answer was obvious.

"Yeah-h-h-h, I can see that." Nick waved his hand at books ranging from climatology to European dance, plus pages of handwritten notes that seemed to be mostly mathematical equations. "But there's nothing here about homunculi."

Angelo scooped the pages into a neat pile. "I told you. There's almost no information available on homunculi."

Nick plopped onto the bed. "So what are we supposed to be looking at from a new angle?"

"I'd like to look at a bag of Doritos from an angle just above my mouth," Carter said. "You have anything to eat around here?"

Angelo pointed to a Tupperware container. Carter opened it to find pieces of cut celery and cherry tomatoes. "Gross." He sniffed. "I'd rather starve."

"Now isn't the time to be thinking about food," Nick snapped.

Carter grunted. "I think better when my stomach isn't growling."

"Mr. Blackham got me thinking with his talk of causality," Angelo said, ignoring Carter's disgusted expression. "Let's go back to the beginning. What events preceded us finding the homunculus in the first place?"

"He swiped my food," Carter said with a wistful expression. "A homunculus after my own heart."

"Okay, good." Angelo wrote *1-Food* on a piece of paper. "Somehow he managed to get into a locked car. Which means he has the ability either to pick locks or squeeze through small spaces."

"The car window was open only half an inch or so," Nick said. "That would be an awfully tight squeeze."

Angelo nodded and added that to the notes. "What happened after that?"

"Well," Nick said, "Carter woke us up. We heard noises. You guys were a bunch of chickens. So I went outside."

"Chicken." Carter rubbed his stomach and groaned.

"After that"—Nick closed his eyes, trying to picture the scene outside the tent—"I was freaked out because I thought Bigfoot was about to . . ." He remembered something that hadn't occurred to him until this very moment and jumped off the bed. "Angelo, pull up the pictures you took at the campsite."

Angelo powered on his iPad and scrolled through his photos until Nick said, "Stop." It was the picture of the huge footprint they'd found outside the tent.

Angelo slapped his head. "I forgot all about this."

"Carter Junior didn't make that," Carter said. "Twenty homunculi together couldn't leave a footprint that big. And there were more of those prints farther into the woods."

Nick studied the footprint. "If Carter Junior didn't leave that footprint, what did?"

"Maybe the homunculus and the Bigfoot hung out," Carter said. "I could totally see Carter Junior going all, 'Dude, wash your toes sometime! Those big feet of

156

yours reek like rotten cabbage.'"

"Hey, what about the movie we made the next morning," Nick said. "The one where we were following the cookies. Did you ever go back and study it?"

Angelo smacked himself again. "I'm the worst scientist ever." He opened his bag and began rummaging through it.

"Speaking of cookies," Carter said, "I'm going to poke around your kitchen and see if you have any human food."

"Here we go." Angelo pulled out the digital camera and connected it to his computer. When he clicked play, a shaky video showed a close-up of Carter—his face so pale that each of his freckles stood out like one of those connect-the-dots games.

There wasn't actually much to see. Angelo talking about the origins of the term *Bigfoot*, Carter searching for cookies, lots of crazy angles on trees. "So much for my career as a cameraman," Nick said.

"Don't touch it," Angelo's on-screen voice said. He stepped in front of the camera, looking down at the three straight lines. He turned to look back at Nick. "This can't be accidental. Are you recording this?"

Although Nick couldn't see himself because the camera had been strapped to his head, he remembered

nodding and moving around for a better look. Sure enough, the camera bobbed up and down, turned for a moment, and then zoomed in on the three lines.

"Hang on." Angelo paused the movie, then slowly began to move it forward.

"What is it?" Nick asked. "Did you see something?"

Angelo stopped the video on the huge redwood they'd found Carter Junior hiding behind. "The same three lines are on the tree."

"Sure," Nick said. Three lines on the left, three on the right, and three on top. "It has to mean three of something. Three homunculi? Three Bigfoot?"

Angelo reversed the video. "Right after you nodded, just before you straightened out the camera, I thought . . ." He froze the film. As Nick had been moving around to get a clear shot, he'd tilted his head. On the screen, everything was sideways; the trees looked like they'd all been blown over in a huge storm. He started to turn his head to see more clearly, but Angelo stopped him.

"Wait. Look at it from this angle. What do you see?" Angelo asked. He was clearly excited about something. But Nick couldn't tell what.

"The same thing we saw then," Nick said. "A bunch of trees. Carter's dirty shoe. And three lines of cookies."

158

"Three lines," Angelo agreed. "But not the vertical lines, three horizontal lines. When you look at it from this direction, the three parallel lines go from left to right instead of up and down." He reached into his backpack and pulled out his math book. He quickly flipped it open to a page and pointed to a symbol just like the one the cookies were arranged in. Nick read the definition written below the symbol.

"Equivalent. Identical to." He looked at Angelo, excitement racing through his body. "What does it mean?"

"Identical to," Angelo muttered to himself. "German. Equivalent. People not acting like themselves." He glanced toward the mirror above his desk and his eyes opened wide. "That's it!" he shouted so loudly that Nick took a step back.

Angelo ran to his closet and began hastily rummaging through books. A moment later he found what he was looking for. He slammed a thick book on the table, checked the table of contents, and opened to a section halfway through.

Nick leaned over to take a look. It was a picture of a man staring at an exact duplicate of himself—like the reflection Angelo had seen of himself, only without the mirror. Beneath the picture was the definition.

Doppelgänger: The spiritual or physical duplicate of a living person. From the German doppel (double) and gänger (goer).

Nick licked his lips and looked at Angelo. "You think?"

Angelo nodded. "The man we saw jogging down the street this morning wasn't Old Man Dashner. It was someone or some*thing* that looked just like him. Ms. Schoepf wasn't Ms. Schoepf. It was her doppelgänger."

Nick had a horrible realization. "The guy who told my mom and me that we were going out to eat wasn't my dad, it was his doppelgänger. That means there's something in my house right now, pretending to be my dad!"

Carter walked into the room munching on a bag of tortilla chips. "Did I miss anything?"

Nick started for the door. But Angelo grabbed him.

"I have to go make sure my parents are okay," Nick said, pulling out of his friend's grasp.

"How will you even know if they're your real parents or not?" Angelo asked. Nick paused. "For all you know, you could be talking to a doppelgänger without even being aware of it."

Carter stopped with a chip halfway to his mouth. "What's a doppelrainer?"

"Doppelgänger," Angelo said. He picked up the book. "Doppelgängers are mythical creatures capable of looking and sounding just like their doubles. Although the German word meaning 'double goer' is fairly recent, history is filled with stories of physical or spiritual duplicates. Ancient Egyptian mythology called it a *ka*. In Norse, it's a *vardøger*. In Finnish folklore, an *Etiäinen* is a spirit double."

"What do these doppelgängers do?" Nick asked. "What do they want with my dad, and Mr. Dashner, and Ms. Schoepf?"

Angelo checked the book. "Not all the stories agree. But according to many accounts, a doppelgänger's appearance can mean bad luck, danger, or even death."

Nick felt like someone had some slammed a lead weight on his chest. He could barely breathe. "My dad's going to die?"

"Come on," Carter said, grabbing a handful of chips. "You're trying to make us believe there are a bunch of what? Evil twins, running around the neighborhood getting ready to kill everyone? Let me guess, they're all riding purple unicorns and blowing party horns."

Angelo glared. "I didn't say they were going to kill

anyone. I said their presence has been known to occur shortly before something bad happens—which, at times, has been death." He flipped the page. "According to several reliable sources, shortly after Abraham Lincoln was elected he looked into a mirror and saw two reflections of himself. One was normal. But the other looked pale and deathlike. His wife thought it was a warning that he would be reelected to a second term but wouldn't live to see the end of it. And that's exactly what happened."

Nick grabbed the book. "Let me see that." He scanned the text. There were dozens of stories of people who saw doubles right before something terrible happened. A guy saw a duplicate of his pregnant wife in France shortly before she lost her baby in England. Percy Bysshe Shelley, the husband of the woman who wrote *Frankenstein*, met his own doppelgänger. The doppelgänger pointed to the Mediterranean Sea, and a few days later, Shelley drowned there. It was scary stuff.

But in at least a few cases, the doubles didn't seem to do any more than cause mischief. "Listen to this," Nick said. "In France there was this thirty-two-year-old schoolteacher named Emilie Sagée. She was writing on the chalkboard when her students saw her exact double

appear standing beside her. The two looked exactly the same, except the doppelgänger wasn't holding any chalk.

"Another time a bunch of girls were in class. When their teacher left the room Sagée's double appeared again—sitting in the teacher's chair. A couple of the girls tried to touch her, but their hands got pushed away by some kind of force."

"How do they know it was a doppelgänger?" Carter scoffed around a mouthful of chips. "Maybe the teachers were just pulling a trick on them."

"Pretty tough to do when the girls could look right out the window and see the real Emilie Sagée planting flowers in the garden. According to this, lots of people reported feeling sick or weak either just before their double appeared or right after he left." He stared at Angelo. "My dad said he wasn't feeling good right after his doppelgänger told us we were going out to dinner. And didn't you say you were feeling tired right about the time Angie and her friends said you were telling them to meet you at your house?"

Angelo dropped into his chair. "I have a doppelgänger. That was who talked to the girls pretending to be me. They must suck some kind of energy from you."

Nick nodded. "Like psychic vampires."

"You guys really buy that mumbo jumbo?" Carter asked. "It's total garbage. But you won't listen to me. I'm sick and tired of you two thinking you're so much smarter than I am. All Carter can do is eat and crack jokes. Well, you know what? I'm the only person in this room with a bit of common sense. You can believe whatever you want, but I'm out of here." He threw the bag of chips on the floor and stomped from the room.

"What was that about?" Angelo asked.

"No clue," Nick said. "Maybe we better go after him."

Before they could, Carter came back into the room. "Man," he said, rubbing his stomach. "I was looking for food when all of a sudden I got major stomach cramps. Totally thought I was gonna hurl. But then it went away and I just felt kind of tired." He glanced down at the bag on the floor. "Who brought the chips?"

CHAPTER 18

I'M NOT SAYING THE BOYS FIGURED OUT SOMETHING I DIDN'T KNOW. ALL RIGHT, MAYBE I AM

"Whoa!" Carter chomped a mouthful of chips. "You're saying I was in here just a minute ago?"

"Not you," Angelo said. "Your doppelgänger. It sucked some energy from you to create itself. That's why you got the stomachache."

"Dude, that is totally awesome!" Carter dug another handful from the bag. "What did I say? Was I like, 'Hey, bro, I'm Carter. What's happening? Do you guys want to par-tay with me and my twin?'"

"It wasn't like that," Nick said. "Mostly it was complaining that we don't take you seriously enough. It said we think we're smarter than you and all you do is eat and crack jokes."

He thought Carter would laugh at the idea, but instead his friend nodded. "It's kind of true, you know. Sounds like my doppelgänger's not all bad."

"What are you talking about?" Nick asked. "Of course it's bad. Doppelgängers cause trouble, and sometimes people even die after their double appears."

Carter dropped the chips. "I'm gonna die?"

"We don't know that," Angelo said. "I wish I'd realized it wasn't you. I could have taken pictures or asked it questions."

"How many of them do you think there are?" Nick asked.

Angelo checked his book. "In the stories it's just one at a time. It could be one here copying many different people. Or it could be a lot."

"We have to get rid of them," Nick said.

Carter raised his hands. "What if we just pretend we don't know anything about them and hope they leave, like Carter Junior?"

"I'm not sure that's an option," Angelo said. "Your double heard us talking about doppelgängers. They're aware that we know about them."

"How do we stop them?" Carter asked. "Do we stab them in the heart with a wooden stake or cut off their heads with a samurai sword?"

"They aren't vampires," Nick said. "And this isn't *Highlander*."

Angelo flipped through his book. "I can't find anything in here about how to kill them. No one even seems to be sure that they're actually alive. The first thing we have to do is figure out how to recognize them. Then we have to find a way to reverse whatever created them in the first place."

"I need to get home and make sure my dad's okay," Nick said.

Carter looked out the window. "The sun's almost down. No way I want to be outside after dark. I bet that's when they're the most powerful."

"I told you, they're not vampires," Angelo said. "But you're right. We should go home. Nick, you check on your dad. I'll do some more research. And Carter . . . you're as smart as any of us. So you do some research too."

Carter gave him an odd look. "All righty, then."

"Keep an eye out for you-know-what," Angelo said, peeking out the door.

All the way home, Nick watched for doppelgängers. Mrs. Wood was out front watering her flowers, which she always did. Mr. Lewis was shooting hoops with his kids. He missed most of his shots, but he wasn't a very

good basketball player, so that probably didn't mean anything.

When Nick got home, Mom was in the living room reading a magazine. He studied her from the kitchen, trying to spot any differences that might reveal her as a double. She looked up from her magazine. "Need something?"

"No," Nick said. "Just saying hi." He tried to sound casual as he asked, "Where's Dad?"

"Upstairs on his computer." She went back to reading, and Nick went to check on his father.

Dad looked up from the computer with a distracted expression when Nick knocked on the door. "Whatchu doin'?" Nick asked.

His dad rubbed his eyes and smiled. But it wasn't the creepy smile from the night before. "Well, I came upstairs to email the company I booked our campground through. I'm *positive* I filled out the right month. But that was twenty minutes ago. I guess I must have dozed off."

"That's cool," Nick said. He searched for any sign of the Evil Dad double, but he didn't really know what he was looking for. If doppelgängers looked exactly like the people they were copying, there would be no way to tell them apart. At least not from their appearance.

He tried going with a different approach. "I was wondering if you might consider increasing my allowance? I was thinking maybe double?"

Dad chortled. "Sure. Just as soon as you start doing twice the chores."

"Fair enough." Nick grinned and went to his room. That was definitely the real Dad.

The next morning, Nick woke up before his alarm had even gone off. He'd been having a nightmare where his mom and dad were snowmen. The sun had been melting them just enough to reveal horrible monsters beneath their snow-white skin. Trying to shake off the memory of the dream, he peeked in on his parents, made sure they were both sleeping normally, and left a note on the kitchen table explaining that he'd gone to Angelo's to catch up on some schoolwork.

Angelo answered the door on the first knock.

"Any luck with your research?" Nick asked.

Angelo led him into his room, where books and papers were spread over every available surface. "Wow!" Nick said admiringly. "You don't do things halfway, do you?"

"We have to know what we're up against," Angelo said. "And, frankly, things don't look good." He grabbed

a handful of notes. "The first thing we have to figure out is where the doppelgängers came from. There seem to be two theories on that. The first is dark magic. Sorcerers are supposed to be able to create doubles of themselves or others using something called bilocation. That's probably out unless you know a sorcerer who's ticked off at you."

"Not at the moment," Nick said.

"Okay, well the other option is that something lured them here."

"Carter Junior," Nick said at once.

Angelo nodded. "That's what I was thinking. This is just guesswork on my part. But let's assume the homunculus and the doppelgängers are both from the same place."

"That could explain the big footprint."

"Maybe," Angelo said. "No one knows exactly what a doppelgänger looks like when it isn't copying a real person. It could be that they are huge. It could even be that all those Bigfoot sightings were really doppelgängers in their native form. If that's true, the theft of the homunculus could have upset them. Or, even worse, it could be, like, attracting them."

Nick pressed a fist to his mouth. "Like bears going after a pot of honey."

"Exactly," Angelo said. "And Mama Bear is hungry."

"Okay, so that means we just find Carter Junior, return him to the woods, and the doppelgängers all go home. Right?"

"It might not be so easy." Angelo turned to his computer and pulled up a map. He pointed to an area of nearly uninterrupted green. "This is where we were camping."

Nick leaned over his shoulder. "Looks like the middle of nowhere."

"Precisely. The only road going in or out is an old logging road. It's normally blocked off, but the rangers were doing some fire prevention. That's the only reason we could even get in."

Nick studied the map. "So it's nearly impossible to get to."

"I believe that's on purpose," Angelo said. "Mr. Grunwald said it was his property. My guess is he knows about the doppelgängers and he's managed to keep them trapped there all this time. It's entirely possible that by taking the homunculus, we broke some kind of barrier. And now that the doppelgängers are out, who says they'll ever want to go back?"

"Tell me that's all the bad news," Nick said, collapsing into a chair.

171

"I wish I could." Angelo picked up another book. "If what I've read is true, doppelgängers take on the physical and mental attributes of their double—with all the knowledge, talents, and strengths of its duplicate. They retain that form until either they or their twin dies."

"So we freed a bunch of them?"

Angelo ran his hands through his hair, making it poke straight up. "Either that or—and this is the part that really worries me—maybe they're replicating."

Nick tried to imagine doppelgängers popping up all over the city. . . . The idea gave him the shivers. "And we don't know how to recognize them, stop them from copying us, or send them back."

"That's pretty much the state of things," Angelo agreed. "For the moment all we can do is watch and hope they get tired of our city. That, and maybe try to figure out where the homunculus is hiding. If we can find it, maybe it will give us some leverage."

The doorbell rang and Nick looked out the window. "That must be Carter."

But when they opened the door, Angie was standing on the front porch.

"What are you doing here?" Nick asked, hoping she hadn't been eavesdropping on their conversation.

Angie shuffled her foot on the porch and looked

away. "I came to say . . . I'm sorry."

"What?" Angelo asked with a look of complete shock. Nick couldn't blame him. In all the years he and Angie had been going to school together, he'd heard her say many things. But "I'm sorry" wasn't one of them.

"I know," Angie said. "I'm a little surprised myself. The thing is, I know you guys have been under a lot of stress with everything that's happened over the last few weeks, and now Carter Junior is missing. So what if you forgot to meet us? It's nothing to lose a friendship over."

Nick wasn't sure they had ever been what he would call friends, but if she was apologizing, it didn't seem right to point that out now. "Okay. And for what it's worth, I'm sorry you guys had to wait for us to get home. Believe it or not, we really were checking on Old Man Dashner."

Angie looked over her shoulder, as if making sure no one was watching. "I heard about that. And don't tell anyone, but I think I know what's going on."

"You do?" Nick asked.

Angie leaned in close and whispered, "Have you ever heard of doppelgängers?"

"Yes," Nick said. He knew Angie and her friends were sharp, but how could they have learned about the

173

doppelgängers when he, Angelo, and Carter had just figured things out themselves? "How could you know that?"

"Never mind that," Angie said. "Have you figured out a way to stop them?"

Nick opened his mouth to say they hadn't yet, when Angelo stepped backward with a gasp of surprise. He looked up at the sky, then down at the porch.

"No," Angelo said. "We have no idea at all. In fact, we're not even sure they really *are* doppelgängers. It could be a myth."

Nick glanced at his friend. What was he talking about?

Angie seemed as surprised as Nick by Angelo's reaction, but she quickly covered it up. "Are you sure? Because if you know how to stop them, Dana, Tiffany, and I could help you. They'll do whatever I tell them."

"Sorry," Angelo said. "We've been busy doing, um, math homework. And we have to get ready for school." He tried to close the door, but Angie put her foot in the way.

She put a hand on Nick's chest—something even more shocking than an apology. "You know, Nick," she said with a gentle smile. "I've always admired you. You're not just smart, but handsome and brave too.

174

Come with me and I'm sure we can figure something out."

All at once, Nick understood what was happening. This wasn't Angie. It was her doppelgänger, spying on them to see what they'd figured out. "We have to go," he said and slammed the door closed, knocking Angie's foot out of the way.

From outside came a screech of anger and a strange popping noise. Like someone had just burst a big balloon. He leaned against the door and turned to Angelo. "How did you know?"

"Remember when Mr. Blackham said he didn't have a shadow of a doubt that we would find a way to identify the problem and fix it?"

Nick tried to remember what the librarian had said. "I guess."

Angelo smiled for the first time that day. "Angie didn't have a shadow."

CHAPTER 19

THIS PART IS TOO CREEPY FOR ME. I'LL GO HAVE ANOTHER HOT DOG

Carter was still wearing his pajamas when Nick and Angelo knocked on his window. "What are you guys doing here so early?" he asked, rubbing his eyes.

"Get dressed," Nick said. "You've got to see what's going on out here."

"It better be free burritos at the Burger Barn if you're making me miss breakfast."

"Trust me," Angelo said. "When you see what we have to show you, you won't feel like eating."

"I'm not sure that's possible." Carter grabbed a T-shirt and jeans. "Meet me out front. But don't let my parents see you. I'm not supposed to have friends over."

"What did you do this time?" Nick asked. Carter

was always in hot water for something. It was almost like he enjoyed being in trouble.

"It's what I *didn't* do. My mom is claiming I ate an entire chocolate cake yesterday that she was saving for guests. Trust me. I'd remember if I did that."

Nick and Angelo shared a look as they walked around to the front of the house. "His doppelgänger?" Nick said.

Angelo nodded. "Now that they know we're on to them, things are only going to get worse."

A few minutes later, Carter snuck out the front door. His shirt was crooked and the laces of one shoe were dragging. "What's so important you're making me lose sleep *and* food?"

"Come here," Nick whispered. He and Angelo walked Carter to the end of his driveway. "Pretend we aren't doing anything."

"Okay," Carter whispered. "What am I supposed to be doing while I pretend I'm *not* doing anything?"

"Look around," Angelo said.

Without being obvious, the three of them glanced about the neighborhood. It was a typical morning. Maybe a little more active than a normal Thursday at this time, but not enough that you would think twice about it. Across the street, a man was pruning his tree.

He nodded at the boys. A pair of kids riding scooters laughed and looked in their direction. A block down, a garbageman was picking up trash. He gave a quick glance their way as he grabbed the next can.

"What am I supposed to be seeing?" Carter asked.

Nick pointed toward Carter's feet. "See your shadow?"

"Of course," Carter said. "You think I'm Peter Pan and it flew away?"

"Now look for theirs," Angelo said.

Carter gazed around, his eyes getting wider and wider. The man pruning looked their way again, his eyes narrow and watchful. He had no shadow. The boys on the scooter were nearly to the corner, but the one who continued to look over his shoulder at them had no shadow either. Even as far away as the garbageman was, it was easy to make out the shadow of his truck and the can he was carrying. The early morning sun stretched them both halfway across the street. But his body cast no shadow at all.

"Holy macaroni," Carter said. "Are they all . . . ?"

"Doppelgängers," Angelo said. "I thought there might be a dozen or so, but we counted three times that many just on the way here. Even assuming they're

more focused around where we live, there have to be hundreds."

"How could there be so many?" Carter asked.

Angelo pulled the boys into a huddle. "Have you guys ever seen an amoeba?"

"Sure," Carter said. "Tiny little things you study under a microscope in science."

Angelo nodded. "Amoebas make more amoebas by splitting in half. One amoeba becomes two. Two become four. Four become eight. After ten splits you're over a thousand. Twenty and you're over a million."

"And they're all watching us," Nick said. Although it wasn't especially cold, Carter shivered. "What are we going to do?"

"Nothing yet," Angelo said. "Right now they're only keeping an eye on us. That means they don't know for sure what we know. But we have to come up with a plan soon, because it's only a matter of time before they decide to do more than watch."

Once they got to school, Nick was relieved to find that Ms. Schoepf and most of the students were their real selves. Only Rob Wells—who raised his hand as soon as class started and admitted he hadn't done any homework for over a week—and a girl who lived down

179

the street from Carter were doppelgängers. At first.

But it quickly became apparent that anytime a student left the room—whether it was to go to the bathroom or to run an errand for the teacher—their doppelgänger immediately showed up. And just before the real kids returned—looking only half awake—their doppelgängers managed to slip out. "They don't want anyone to see two of the same people at the same time," Nick whispered.

"According to some of the stories I read, the worst thing that can happen is coming face-to-face with your own double," Angelo said. "It almost always means your death is imminent."

"I don't want to see any of them," Carter whispered, his eyes on the same piece of paper he'd pretended to take notes on all day. "It freaks me out the way they keep watching us."

When the final bell rang, the three of them were the first ones out of their seats. But they were barely out the door when a figure stepped in front of them. "May I have a word with you boys?"

It was Mrs. Carpenter, their principal. Ordinarily Mrs. Carpenter was a funny woman with a quick smile. She dressed up as the Cat in the Hat for Reading Week, sang the school announcements over the intercom, and

rode her bike to school when the weather was nice. But now her expression was stern, her eyes dark.

Nick glanced quickly toward her feet. No shadow. "I'd like to," he said. "But I have to get home right away."

"This will only take a moment," the principal's doppelgänger said. "But if you'd rather have me call your parents and explain that you are failing all your subjects . . ."

Nick looked at his friends. "I guess we have a minute."

The doppelgänger led the boys into a dead-end hallway where the janitor's closet and supply room were located. It was currently empty. She stared down at them with a mocking smile. "Don't pretend you don't recognize me."

"Of course we do," Carter said, his voice shaking. "You're the p-p-principal."

"Am I?" For just a moment, Mrs. Carpenter's face disappeared. Behind it was rough, dark skin. A black mouth opened up in a grin that split the face nearly in half. Above the mouth there was nothing. No eyes. No nose. Nothing but flat, blank skin.

Nick backed away, a squeak of terror forcing its way out of his throat. Then the principal's face was there again.

"Now will you admit to knowing who, and what, I am?"

All three boys nodded numbly.

"Very good. Then I will tell you what you are going to do. First, you are no longer needed at school. Your duplicates will take your places. They are superior to you in every respect, so no one will miss you. Second, you will not try to interfere with us in any way. You are going to stop trying to learn about us. In particular you will stay away from your friend at the library."

Nick's throat felt locked closed, but he forced himself to speak. "What if we don't? What if, instead, we tell everyone we know about you?"

"Especially Mr. Blackham," Carter said.

The principal's face disappeared again—her blank, eyeless skin terrifying in a way no eyes could ever be. "That would be a very big mistake," the gaping black mouth said, flashing ragged pieces of what looked like rotten black teeth. "No one would believe you and terrible things would begin happening to those you love. *Painful* things. Do I make myself clear?"

All three boys nodded.

Angelo, clutching his notebook so tightly his fingers were white, swallowed. "W-what do you want?"

The doppelgänger leered, its mouth dark and wet,

before turning back into the principal. "I thought you would have understood by now. What we want . . . is to become you."

Nick's insides turned to ice. "If you become us, what do we become?"

The principal smiled gently, but Nick knew the hidden black mouth's grin was wide. "Why, you become fainter and fainter—growing more insubstantial by the day—until eventually . . ." She flicked her fingers and a cloud of black dust floated to the ground. "Poof."

With that, she turned and walked away. Nick, Angelo, and Carter stood like ice sculptures of boys until the fake principal disappeared around the corner. A second later there was the same popping sound Nick had heard after he closed the door on Angie. Still shaking, he edged to the corner and peeked around. There hadn't been time for the doppelgänger to reach the next door, but she was gone.

"Let's get out of here," Carter said.

Staying out of sight as much as possible, they took the back way out of the school, cut through a row of bushes, and came out behind the church on the other side.

"What are we gonna do?" Carter said.

Nick's hands felt ice-cold. He rubbed them, trying to

create a little warmth. "We have to go to Mr. Blackham. It's our only chance."

"Didn't you hear that lady?" Carter said. "Don't tell anyone. Especially not him. Do you really want to find out what the doppelgängers will do to your mom and dad? To my sisters and little brother?"

Nick didn't even want to think about that.

"That wasn't any lady," Angelo said. "Did you see what was behind her face?"

Carter rubbed his arms, which were covered in goose bumps. "I think I'll be seeing it for the rest of my life."

"We have to do something," Nick said. "We can't just let them get away with it."

"We will," Angelo said. "But we need time to come up with a plan. The good news is that if they're warning us to stay away, there must still be a way to stop them." He turned to Carter. "The more I think about it, the more I believe finding that homunculus is the key to stopping the doppelgängers. I need you to find it—I mean him. Where would you go if you were Carter Junior?"

Carter's jaw tightened. "I'll think of a way to find him."

"And Nick," Angelo said. "Try to find out if your

parents suspect anything. If any adult other than Mr. Blackham might believe us, it's them. But make sure you don't spill anything that might put them in danger. We ask for help only if it's a last resort. Let's meet at the top of Dinosaur Hill tomorrow morning at six. Tell your parents we're going to the school for an early study session. Try not to let anyone see you on the way there."

"What are you going to do?" Nick asked.

Angelo rubbed his temples. "I'm going to flex my strongest muscle. My brain."

CHAPTER 20

AH, YES.
MUCH BETTER.
SORRY ABOUT THE
MUSTARD STAIN

Nick lay awake almost all night, worried sick about what was happening and how little he could do about it. Every time he managed to doze off, he thought he heard something creeping around the hallway outside his door and jerked awake.

When the alarm went off at five thirty, he turned it off and rolled out of bed. He dressed as quietly as possible, skipping a shower and anything else that might wake his parents.

He desperately wanted to go into their room and tell them everything. To have his mom and dad tell him it was going to be okay. But after beating around the bush all night, he was sure they had no clue anything out of the ordinary was happening. If he told them what he knew, not only would they probably not believe him, but they'd also be in danger.

Then again, weren't they already in danger? If the doppelgängers planned on becoming the people they had copied, they wouldn't stop with Nick and his friends. It would be like that old movie *Invasion of the Body Snatchers*, where no one knows the population is being replaced by aliens until it's too late.

No matter how he considered it, there didn't seem to be any good answer. He wrote another note to his parents, left it on the table, and slipped out the kitchen door. As soon as he was outside, he peeked around the bushes. Sure enough, Mrs. Wood was in front of her house watering her flowers. Except if you watched closely enough, you could see that she was actually letting the water run onto her lawn instead of her garden. And despite the morning sun, her body did not cast a shadow. Where was the real Mrs. Wood? Sick in bed? Or inside her house in a kind of daze, slowly fading away?

Fortunately he had planned for this. Staying low, he snuck through his backyard into the bushes behind the Chens' house. He pulled his bike out from where he'd hidden it next to their shed. Mrs. Wood, watching the front of his house, would think either that he'd stayed home or that she'd somehow missed him. Either way, she couldn't report where he'd gone.

As soon as he had his bike, he reached into his backpack and pulled out a dark hoodie, sunglasses, and a baseball cap. Let anyone try to figure out who he was under all that. Even with the disguise, though, he realized someone might be able to recognize his bike. So he took the long route to the park, avoiding houses where he could see anyone outside.

With all the extra turns and doubling back, it was nearly a quarter after six by the time he pumped his bike to the top of Dinosaur Hill. Angelo was waiting for him under the big oak tree. "I was worried you weren't going to make it," he said.

Nick pulled down his hood but left on his cap and sunglasses. "I rode halfway across the city trying to make sure no one recognized me. Where's Carter?"

"I haven't seen him," Angelo said. "You don't think he got scared and decided not to come, do you?"

"He'll be here," Nick said. Carter might have his faults, but he didn't let his friends down.

As they waited, Nick asked Angelo, "Have you thought of a plan?"

Angelo fiddled with his backpack, which seemed

more full than usual. "You mean a formal plan with dates, times, and directions? That kind of plan?"

"Any kind of plan," Nick said. "Even one that might not work."

Angelo shook his head. "No."

This was going to be a long day. In the distance, Nick noticed a little girl riding her bike toward the park. "Get down," he said. "Someone's coming."

He and Angelo pulled their bikes behind the tree and dropped into the grass. Nick wondered why a girl would be out riding her bike at this time of morning. She should be having breakfast and getting ready for school. She seemed to be having a difficult time keeping her bike balanced. It looked like it was too small for her. Under her pink dress, her knees pumped up and down. And with each turn of the pedals, the bike wobbled left and right.

"What's with her hair?" Angelo said. "It looks all white and stringy."

"Yeah," Nick agreed. "It's mean to say, but that might be the ugliest girl I've ever seen." He kept waiting for the girl to turn into the driveway of one of the houses near the park. But she never did. "Look out," he hissed. "She's coming right toward us."

He buried his face in the grass, afraid to look up.

He could hear the heavy breathing of someone getting closer. The *tick, tick, tick* of bike spokes grew louder until it finally stopped, right on top of them by the sound of it.

"Are you two supposed to be hiding, or kissing the ground?" a voice asked.

Nick raised his head just in time to see the ugly girl pull off a white wig, revealing black-and-white-striped hair beneath it. She yanked off her pink dress, unrolled the jeans that had been turned up to her knees, and flung the girls' bike to the ground. "Stupid thing!"

"Carter?" Nick burst out laughing. "What are you doing in a dress? And is that your little sister's bike?"

"What does it look like I'm doing?" Carter grumbled, giving the bike a hard kick. "They had my house completely surrounded. It was the only way I could get out without them recognizing me."

Angelo beamed. "Brilliant! I've never seen such an amazing disguise in my life."

"Yeah, well, next time *you* try riding the bike of an eight-year-old girl a mile and a half up a hill. It stinks." Carter tried to look angry, but couldn't completely hide his smile. He picked up the stringy white wig. "My mom's gonna kill me when she sees what I did to her

mop." He flopped to the ground and leaned against the trunk of the tree. "Please tell me one of you thought to bring food. I'm dying."

"As a matter of fact, I did," Angelo said. He opened his pack and took out a bag of Reese's Peanut Butter Cups Miniatures and a six-pack of Mountain Dew.

Carter moaned with delight and held out his hands. "Manna from heaven. Gimme, gimme, gimme."

Nick couldn't help smiling as he watched Carter fill his mouth with chocolate and wash it down with soda. Even the worst of circumstances were a little more bearable when you were with friends.

When Carter had finished his second can of Mountain Dew and at least fifteen miniatures, Angelo asked, "Have you given any thought to where Carter Junior might have gone?"

Carter burped so loudly his cheeks ballooned out and nodded. "Yes. I thought about it all night, and the answer is . . . he wouldn't."

"Huh?" Nick said.

Angelo tapped his notebook impatiently. "What kind of answer is that?"

"He wouldn't have left," Carter said. "If I was six inches tall and someone offered me free soda and

candy, all the comic books I could read, and a comfortable room with no school or chores, I would never, ever leave. Period."

"But that's *you*," Angelo said. "We're talking about a homunculus."

"A homunculus who could change into anyone, but spent most of his time as me," Carter said. He crossed the first two fingers on his right hand. "We were like this. And I'm telling you, he wouldn't have left."

Angelo shook his head, but Nick was beginning to understand. "Carter's right. Carter Junior spent the most time around him, and some of that must have rubbed off. Carter would never leave that kind of situation."

"What are you saying?" Angelo asked.

"I'm saying we were right the first time. Carter Junior didn't run away. He was taken."

Angelo folded his arms and frowned. "You still think it was Angie?"

"No," Nick said. As easy as it would be to blame Angie, he didn't think she or her friends would have done something like that. He looked down the hill into Mr. Dashner's backyard and something occurred to him. "Do you guys remember when we were talking to Old Man Dashner and he said something about us

192

sneaking through his yard two nights before?"

"The only thing I remember is running for my life," Carter said.

But Angelo nodded. "I remember that."

"It would have been the same night Carter Junior disappeared," Nick said.

"And since it wasn't us sneaking through his backyard, who was it?" Angelo asked.

Carter stood up. "If someone lived on the other side of this hill, Old Man Dashner's yard would be the easiest way to get to my house without being seen."

Nick spoke out loud, trying to put together his thoughts. "It would have to be someone who lives over by the school, in the rich part of town. Someone who knew we had the homunculus and wanted it. Someone who . . ."

Suddenly he had it. "The doppelgängers came after our families early on because we took the homunculus. But if the homunculus was what attracted them in the first place, the first person they would have looked for was the person who had Carter Junior. And the first person who got sick and started acting weird was—"

"Kimber Tidwell," Carter said. "She saw Carter Junior on the playground. And she went to the nurse the next morning."

"But she came back a few minutes later and told her friends off about the hats, which was totally unlike her," Angelo said. "I think you're right. I think it's her. I know where she lives. She should be leaving for school any minute, and both her parents work."

Carter jumped up and grabbed his sister's bike. "It's time for Operation Little Guy."

CHAPTER 21

I DON'T HAVE A SHADOW OF A DOUBT WHO IT IS

DOUBT WHO IT IS

They had barely reached the bottom of the hill—Angelo leading the way, Nick close behind him, and Carter struggling to keep from crashing his little sister's bike—when the sky, which had been clear all week, began to fill with threatening, dark gray clouds.

"Tell me . . . you've . . . got an . . . umbrella in . . . that pack," Carter puffed.

"Sorry," Angelo said. "I couldn't think of everything."

Between his dark sunglasses and the heavy clouds, it nearly looked like night to Nick. He glanced over his shoulder, checking on Carter. "You okay back there?"

"Peachy," Carter gasped. "But if I biff it, you have to

promise to take my lifeless body back to my parents."

"Deal," Nick said.

A few minutes later, big fat drops began to plummet from the sky. It was the kind of rain that felt like someone flicking you with their finger over and over. Nick took off his baseball cap and slowed enough to let Carter catch up with him. "This will help keep you at least a little bit dry."

"You keep it," Carter said, his face red with exertion. "I like . . . the . . . rain."

Nick pushed the cap toward him anyway. "I have my hoodie. Besides, it will help disguise your hair. Anyone who sees that skunk head will know it's you right away."

Carter took the hat. "Yankees? I hate the Yankees." But he shoved it on his head anyway.

Up ahead, Angelo turned right and pulled his bike into some trees at the edge of a lawn half the size of a football field.

"No wonder Kimber's so popular," Carter said. "If she loses one friend, she can just buy two more."

"Money doesn't buy happiness," Angelo said.

Carter wiped the rain off his face with the sleeve of his T-shirt. "True, but it buys cool things. And cool things make me happy. That and, you know, food."

Angelo shook his head. "I'm not sure she's left for school yet. Let's hide our bikes here and sneak around back. We don't want any of the neighbors to see us waiting."

One by one, they hid their bikes in the small grove of trees and crept along the side of the yard toward the back of the house. "We really need some cool music for this," Carter whispered. "Kind of a thing song. Like something from the *Avengers* movie."

"It's called a *theme* song, not a *thing* song," Angelo said.

"Ahh, same *theme*," Carter said, chuckling at his own joke.

At least the rain was beginning to let up. Nick was shivering inside his hoodie, and he couldn't imagine how cold Carter must be. Halfway to the backyard, he began not to feel so good. "Hang on," he whispered, clutching his stomach.

"You okay?" Carter asked.

"Yeah." He put his hand over his mouth to stifle a burp. "I think the Mountain Dew is coming back on me."

"It's nearly as good the second time around," Carter said.

Nick groaned. "That's totally disgusting, man."

He pressed his face to the cool, wet grass, and after a few minutes felt better. "Okay," he said. "We can go now."

By the time they found a hiding place behind the Tidwells' mansion, the rain had stopped completely and the sky was beginning to clear. Nick wiped his mouth. "Remind me to stick with water next time," he said. "That Mountain Dew has a kick."

"Look." Angelo pointed to the back door, where Rebel Benson had just shown up. The boys watched as Rebel knocked on the door. A minute later, Kimber came out wearing a fluffy pink skirt with a poodle on the side and a matching pink beret.

"I wouldn't let my dog go out dressed like that," Carter said.

"I wouldn't let my dog go out dressed in anything," Angelo said.

"If my dog looked like either one of you, I'd shave its rear and walk it backward," Nick said. It was an old joke, and a pretty dumb one at that, but it made them all bust up anyway—hands pressed to their mouths to cover the noise.

"Let's go," Angelo said when the girls were out of sight.

"How are we going to get inside?" Nick asked.

Angelo looked quickly around to make sure no one was watching and started toward the house. "We'll try the door first. If I know Kimber, she didn't bother locking it. Girls like her never even think someone might break into their house. If it's locked we'll start checking windows."

Sure enough, when Angelo tried the knob it turned easily. "Move fast and don't touch anything," he said. He glanced back at his friends. "Remember, the goal is to—" Suddenly his voice cut off and his eyes grew huge behind his thick glasses. Without a word, he dove forward and tackled Carter to the ground.

"Get off me," Carter howled, struggling under Angelo's weight.

"What are you doing?" Nick demanded. He tried to pull Angelo off Carter, but the two of them were locked tightly together.

Angelo looked up, his face covered in sweat. "Help me hold on to him," he gasped, narrowly avoiding a kick from Carter's knee. "He doesn't have a shadow. He's a doppelgänger."

It took a moment for Nick to realize what Angelo had just said. When he did, he dove to the ground, grabbing one of the doppelgänger's arms and pinning one of its legs with the weight of his body.

199

"Are you guys crazy?" the doppelgänger yelled, squirming and twisting.

"Nice try," Angelo snarled. "But we know what you are."

"I'm not a doppelgänger," the Carter look-alike said. "Don't you guys recognize your own friend?"

"Are you sure it's not him?" Nick asked, struggling to keep his grip on the creature's sweaty arm. "It sounds like Carter."

"Of course it's me," the doppelgänger cried. "For pity's sake, I've been with you guys all morning."

Angelo grunted. "It's trying to trick you. It doesn't have a shadow. Lift it partway up and I'll show you."

Still holding both of its arms, Nick and Angelo lifted the doppelgänger to a sitting position. Angelo was right. There was no shadow at all.

"See," the doppelgänger said. "I told you I have a . . ." It looked down with an expression of surprise that seemed so real, Nick nearly believed it. "Where did it go? Where in the name of secret sauce is my shadow?"

"The doppelgänger must have taken Carter when we were riding our bikes here," Angelo said. "Were you watching him the whole time?"

Nick shook his head. "I checked on him a couple of times. But not all the way."

"Come on, guys," the doppelgänger begged. "You have to believe me. I'm Carter. If I was a doppelgänger I'd do that whole disappearing-face routine and bite you with my huge mouth."

"Not if you were trying to lure us into revealing our plans," Angelo said.

The doppelgänger stopped struggling, but Nick kept a tight grip on it. "You're good," he said. "If it wasn't for the whole shadow thing, I'd never guess you weren't the real Carter."

As they were trying to figure out what to do with the creature, the last clouds blew away and the sun came out.

"Look!" the doppelgänger said, pointing to the ground. "See, I *do* have a shadow."

Nick squinted. The doppelgänger was right. There was a shadow. It was so light you could barely see it. A very pale gray, unlike the much darker shadows of Nick and Angelo. But it was definitely a shadow. "Carter?"

"Yes," the doppelgänger said, struggling to its feet. "It's me. And I am never going on a search-and-rescue operation with you guys again."

"I think it really *is* him," Nick said, releasing Carter's arm. "But what's wrong with his shadow? It's like it almost doesn't exist."

Angelo reluctantly began to let go of Carter. "How do you feel?"

"How do you think I feel?" Carter yanked his arm out of Angelo's grip. "I've had it with you two never trusting me."

"It's not that we don't trust you," Nick said. "It's just . . ."

"No." Carter shook his head. "My doppelgänger was right. You guys think all I ever do is eat and joke around. And you know what? I'm sick and tired of it." He turned and stomped through the door. "I'm rescuing Carter Junior by myself if I have to."

Nick wished there was something he could say. Maybe Carter was right, though. They hadn't trusted him—not when he'd said he'd heard something outside the tent, not when the homunculus escaped, and not now. It was a pretty lousy way to treat a friend. He rubbed the back of his neck and followed Carter into the house.

"Anybody home?" Carter shouted.

"Shhh," Angelo hissed. "What are you doing?"

"Would you rather find out someone's home now or when we're halfway through ransacking their house?" Carter asked.

"We're not ransacking anything," Angelo whispered. "We're finding the homunculus. Grabbing it and getting out."

With all the lights off, the big house was dark and more than a little creepy. "They don't have a dog, do they?" Nick whispered.

Angelo paused and looked back. "I don't think so."

"This is not how it works in *Mission Impossible*," Carter muttered. "Where are the night-vision goggles and gloves that let you climb walls?"

"Actually," Angelo whispered back, "I have a pair of night-vision goggles in my backpack. But I'm hoping we don't have to use them."

When they reached the stairs, Angelo motioned up. "I'm guessing her room is on the second floor."

Nick wasn't sure why they were being so quiet when they'd already determined no one was home. But he stuck to the side of the staircase anyway to keep from making the steps squeak. At the top of the stairs, Angelo tried the first door. It was a music room with a violin on a stand, a flute, and a grand piano.

"I always wanted to play the flute," Carter said. "Like those guys in the Revolutionary War. I'm a Yankee Doodle Dandy."

"Be quiet," Angelo said with an irritated look back.

Carter glared. "Some people have no appreciation for music."

Nick shook his head. It was like the two of them were intentionally trying to get on each other's nerves.

The second door opened into what appeared to be a guest room. Nick had never seen a bedroom so clean in his life. It looked like if you dropped so much as a feather, a dozen alarms would go off. Come to think of it, they were lucky that an alarm hadn't been set.

The third room they checked was so pink it nearly made Nick's eyes water.

"This is it," Carter whispered. "Seriously, her parents should be arrested for child abuse. This much pink is illegal in at least twenty states."

"Okay," Angelo said. "We have no idea if she's keeping the homunculus here or somewhere else. But this is as good a place as any to start. You check the closet, I'll look under the bed, and—"

"Carter Junior, are you in here, buddy?" Carter called.

Angelo shot him a dirty look. But instantly a muffled copy of Carter's voice called back, "Are you in here, buddy?"

With a shout of joy, Carter ran to a large cedar chest

and threw it open.

"I'm hungry!" the homunculus called happily from inside a cage of tightly woven wire mesh.

Carter grabbed the cage, fiddled with a latch that was located where the tiny creature couldn't reach it from the inside, and opened the door. The homunculus leaped for his shoulder, but it missed and barely managed to catch the front of his shirt.

"Are you okay?" Carter asked.

As Angelo knelt down to take a look, the homunculus gave a raspy cough. "He doesn't look good," Angelo said. "We need to get him back to the woods as soon as possible."

"How are we going to do that?" Nick asked. "It's not like we can ride our bikes there."

Angelo grabbed his iPad and did a quick search. "There's a bus that leaves in two hours. If we're careful, the doppelgängers shouldn't have any clue we've left."

"I wouldn't count on that," a voice said.

Nick spun around to find three figures blocking the doorway.

"Nice to meet you in person," a familiar voice said. The figure stepped forward and Nick felt the blood drain from his face. He was looking at an exact copy of himself—from his clothes to his face, to the way his

205

hair stuck up a little in the back.

Except it *wasn't* him. There was something about the eyes staring back at him—something evil and hungry—that made him want to turn away. All at once he could understand why people had died after seeing their doppelgängers. It was like seeing a dark reflection of yourself, a piece of you that until that very moment had been hidden from view.

Angelo and Carter's doppelgängers stepped into the room as well. They eyed the three boys and grinned. "Sorry, guys. The game is over. And you lose."

CHAPTER 22

THE ONLY THING THAT WOULD MAKE THIS CHAPTER MORE EXCITING IS ONE OF THOSE GREAT CHASE SCENES WHERE . . . OH, WAIT

Nick tried to speak but the words wouldn't come. "Give us the homunculus," Evil Nick said.

Carter hugged Carter Junior to his chest. "You can't have him."

"*You can't have him*," Carter's doppelgänger repeated in a whiny voice. "Dude. No wonder Angie and her friends don't want to hang with you. You're pathetic."

Evil Angelo elbowed Evil Carter. "I hate to say it, but I think your double is even more annoying than you are."

Evil Carter sneered. "Well, you should know everything there is about annoying. You wrote the book on annoying, and then read it until you had it memorized."

"Would you two quit arguing," Nick's doppelgänger said. He looked at Nick. "Why you choose to hang around these two is beyond me. Seriously, they are like a couple of little old ladies in a grocery store arguing over who gets the last cantaloupe. You know?"

Nick nearly nodded, before remembering who he was talking to.

"I thought you three were supposed to be taking our places in school," Angelo said.

His double took off his glasses and polished them on his shirt exactly the way Angelo always did. "Technically, we were there until just a minute ago. But a kindly neighbor lady across the street, who happens to be one of us, spotted your bikes out front. So we thought we'd *pop* in."

"You guys better back off," Nick said, his tongue feeling twice as big as normal.

"Or what?" Evil Nick asked with a mocking smile. "Are you going to call your mommy? I'll bet if I go to your house right now I can get her to kiss me on the head and feed me pancakes."

Nick raised his fist and, like a mirror image, his double raised his. He took a step to his right and at almost the same time, his doppelgänger matched his

movement. He cut back to the left and Evil Nick was right there.

"Look," Evil Nick said. "We know all about the things you guys have done in the past. We have your memories too. But what you need to realize is, that's all over now. We think like you, we act like you, we look like you. And in another twenty-four hours, we will *be* you."

Evil Carter pointed at Carter and laughed. "What's freaking hilarious is that if you guys had gotten here a day earlier—"

"Stop talking so much!" Evil Angelo scolded. "Go check the kitchen. Maybe there's a bag of doggie treats for you to snack on."

"Why don't you go read a book?" Evil Carter said. "Try looking up the Latin translation of know-it-all."

Nick's double raised his hands as if to say, *How do you put up with this?* "Here's the thing. By now you know that we are what you call doppelgängers—although we have existed long before that name."

"You might want to write this down in your monster notebook," Evil Angelo said. "Which, by the way, I'm planning on keeping up when you're gone."

Angelo frowned, but he unzipped his backpack and

took out his notebook anyway.

Evil Nick shook his head. "In the past we were spread across the world, appearing now and then to people, watching them, warning them, occasionally causing a little mischief. But mostly trying to teach them."

"Teach them what?" Carter growled. "How to be buttheads?"

"Buttheads," Carter Junior repeated weakly.

Angelo's evil double held a hand out toward Angelo. "Please tell your companions that if they continue to interrupt, we will never get through this. But use small words or they might not understand."

"I don't tell my friends what to do," Angelo said.

Evil Angelo shook his head. "Another reason your attempt to stop us has always been doomed to failure. Very well, let's make this brief. In the past, our kind tried to teach your race to stop hiding their true feelings— to let their inner personalities come out. Not everyone liked our message. They started rumors about us, blamed us for their own misfortunes, and trapped us in 'sanctuaries' like the one where you discovered us."

"Luckily, you doofuses opened the door," Carter's doppelgänger said.

"I told you to zip your lips," Evil Angelo told him.

Evil Carter snorted. "And I told you to stick your

210

head in a toilet. If it would even fit."

"What door?" Angelo asked.

His doppelgänger brushed the question away like swatting a fly. "It's not important. What *is* important is that we're free now, and we're not going back. Trying to teach you didn't work. So instead, we're going to become you. It's already happening. Once we finish becoming, you disappear."

Nick balled up his fists. "We didn't know we were letting you out or we never would have done it. And we're going to find a way to send you jerks back where you belong."

"Dream on," Evil Nick said. "It's too late to send us back. And even if it wasn't, you weenies would never have a chance. Haven't you noticed you're losing your strength? Your shadows are disappearing; you're feeling sick, tired. Trust me, you're the ones who are going where you belong—bye-bye."

"I wouldn't have put it in those exact terms," Evil Angelo said. "But he *is* right. We are replacing you. Once we scrape out all the things that get in the way— what you call being polite, civilized, and kind—we will dominate the rest of your species, then the world." He held out his hand. "So leave the homunculus here and you can go."

211

Carter grabbed the metal cage and held it over his head like a weapon. "We aren't leaving here without Carter Junior."

"If you knew he was here, why didn't you come and get him yourselves?" Nick asked. It didn't make sense. "What do you need him for?"

"We don't *need* him," Evil Carter said. "Little dude's about to croak anyway. It's just that—"

Evil Angelo whirled around, his jaw tight. "I told you to stop talking!"

While Evil Angelo was facing Evil Carter, the real Angelo slipped his hand into the backpack he had unzipped moments before. "While it does appear to be true that you have both our physical and mental capabilities, there is one thing you do not have."

"And what would that be?" Evil Angelo asked, his tone and expression clearly indicating he couldn't imagine anything he didn't have.

Angelo pulled a small metal can from his pack, flipped the cap off with his thumb, and shot a cone of mist at the Evil Twins. A thick vapor filled the air around the doppelgängers and they immediately fell back, coughing and gagging. "Pepper spray."

"I have something you don't have too!" Carter shouted. He flung the cage he'd been holding and it

bounced off Evil Carter's head with a loud *twang-g-g*.

"Put these on," Angelo said, pulling out three surgical masks. "And cover your eyes."

As Nick put on the mask, his doppelgänger stumbled toward him, eyes streaming. Nick grabbed one of Kimber's chairs and swung it like a baseball bat. It caught Evil Nick just at belt level, doubling him over. "Now who feels sick?" he shouted.

"Run!" Angelo yelled. He covered his eyes and ran past the reeling doppelgängers.

"Ignore the smell," Carter told the homunculus, tucking it inside his shirt. "I forgot to shower this morning."

Nick covered his eyes with his hands and ran after his friends into the hall. As soon as they were past the pepper spray cloud, they turned and raced down the stairs.

"Get the bikes," Angelo shouted. They charged out the door and ran toward the front yard. Behind them, in the house, Nick could hear furious shouts and pounding footsteps.

"Look out!" Carter yelled.

Nick turned around just in time to see an old woman coming at him with a rake. "What are you boys doing in that house?" the woman shouted, lunging toward him.

A wave of guilt surged through Nick and he nearly stopped before Angelo yelled, "No shadow, she's not real."

Knowing it wasn't a real woman he was doing it to, but feeling terrible about it anyway, Nick ducked under the swinging rake and stuck out his foot. He caught the doppelgänger right in the ankles. "Whup!" the creature squawked, throwing out its hands and flying forward.

In the brief glimpse he got before he turned back toward his bike, Nick thought it looked sort of like Superman leaping into flight—if Superman was a seventy-year-old woman with a bathrobe for a cape. Based on the thump and gasp behind him, he had to assume the flight hadn't lasted long.

Carter was the first one to his bike. He yanked it up by the handlebars and jumped on without losing a step. Angelo was a few feet behind him as he threw his pack over the handlebars of his bike and kicked off. But with a faster bike, he quickly caught up.

Across the street, a muscular man with a big belly came running out of his house. He was wearing only a T-shirt and a pair of boxers. His hairy legs pumped as his bare feet slapped against the ground, but like the old woman, he had no shadow. "Stop, you punks!" he yelled, running into the street.

Angelo managed to pass the doppelgänger, but Carter wasn't fast enough to make it. Instead he dropped his head, aimed his girl's bike directly at the man, and screamed, "Banzai!"

Nick—who had just reached his bike—watched in horrified fascination. Pedaling like a madman, head lowered, feet a blur, Carter charged. At the last minute, the man realized his danger and tried to turn aside, but it was too late.

Carter and the doppelgänger collided in the dead center of the street. It was like watching a speeding Volkswagen run into a mostly stationary SUV. The girls' bike flipped end over end into the air. With a *woof* of dismay the man fell backward. Carter, his feet still trying to pedal, launched like a skunk-haired rocket. He somersaulted once, ducked his head, and landed directly on the man's belly, before bouncing like a kid on a trampoline and miraculously landing on his feet.

Nick snatched his bike and rode up next to Carter. "Get on!" Carter grabbed his shoulders and jumped onto the back of Nick's bike. "Are you okay?" Nick asked, racing to catch up with Angelo.

"Never better!" Carter grinned. "Who knew bellies were so bouncy?"

"We have to get out of the neighborhood," Angelo said.

"Which way?" Nick gasped for air. Riding with Carter on the bike was twice as hard as riding by himself, but it was more than that. Although it was still morning, it felt like he'd been going all day.

Behind them, a black sedan raced around the corner, its tires squealing. "Right!" Angelo shouted, nearly colliding with Nick as the two cut around the corner.

The sound of the car's engine grew louder. Nick felt Carter turn to look back. "Faster!" Carter yelled. "It's going to run us over!"

Nick pedaled as hard he could, switching the bike into its highest gear to get all the speed possible. At the next corner, the boys jumped the curb and cut across a lawn. Behind them, the car screeched its brakes, trying to make the turn.

Ahead of them, another car pulled into the street. It was a police car, its blue and red lights flashing. Nick felt a flicker of hope. Maybe someone had seen the kids running and called the cops. The police wouldn't believe their story, but they wouldn't let anyone take them either. He started toward the car, but Angelo shook his head. "He could be a doppelgänger."

"Where do we go?" Nick said. Behind them the

black sedan was coming fast. In front of them, the police car gunned its engine.

"There!" Carter pointed to an opening between two yards. It was a bike path—too narrow for cars, but perfect for the boys. They turned into it just as the cars skidded to a halt behind them.

"We made it!" Carter shouted. But his excitement quickly disappeared as they came out on the other side. The street was filled with men and women—some on foot, others on bikes. Three quick pops sounded and the boys' Evil Twins appeared in front of them.

"Whoa!" Carter gasped as the boys braked their bikes. "How did you do that?"

Evil Angelo clucked his tongue. "I told you your plan was doomed to failure."

Nick searched for some way out, but there were too many people—all of them closing in. Behind them, the bike path was blocked off by the police car. "Raise your hands and surrender," the policeman called over his loudspeaker.

Just then, an SUV came screaming around the corner. Nick recognized it at once. The back door flew open and his dad yelled, "Get in!"

Throwing down their bikes, the boys darted away from the crowd and dove into the backseat of the car.

Nick's dad punched the gas and smoke billowed from the tires as the SUV shot away.

"How did you find us?" Nick asked, clutching his hand to his chest. His heart felt like it was going to pound straight out of his rib cage.

Dad grinned into the rearview mirror as he turned a corner. "It wasn't easy."

"You're not going to believe this," Carter panted. "But those people behind us weren't real. They were doppelgängers."

"Oh, I believe it," Dad said. He touched a panel beside his seat, and the back doors locked. "I believe all of it." He raised his hand and held it toward the windshield, making sure the boys could see.

Nick gasped. There was no shadow.

CHAPTER 23

IF YOU LIKED THE FIRST TRIP, THIS ONE WILL SLAY YOU

"You're a doppelgänger," Nick said.

His father's double nodded. "Guilty as *changed*."

Carter grabbed the door handle, but the door wouldn't open. He tried the window, but that wouldn't open either. The doppelgänger had turned on the child locks.

"Where's my real dad?" Nick demanded.

Evil Dad drove straight through a red light without stopping and cars swerved to avoid them. "He and your mother are resting peacefully. They've both been feeling a little worn out this morning."

Below the seat, where the doppelgänger couldn't see, Nick made a spraying motion to Angelo. If they could pepper-spray Evil Dad, they might be able to reach the locks and escape.

Angelo moved to reach for his backpack before looking wildly around. Nick realized he'd left it on the handlebars of his bike. The pepper spray, along with any other gadgets he might have brought, were gone.

They pulled onto the freeway, cutting in front of a truck driver, who blared his horn. Nick looked out the window. "Where are you taking us?"

"Somewhere you three will be out of the way, while we finish becoming you and your neighbors," Evil Dad said.

Nick felt sick. It was the worst feeling in the world to look into the face of your own father and know that he was planning to destroy you—even if inside you knew that it wasn't really him.

Angelo shook his head. "You doppelgängers keep saying there's nothing we can do to stop you. So why bother chasing us?"

Evil Dad turned on the radio and began to hum. "I think that's enough talking for now."

Huddled in the backseat, Nick, Angelo, and Carter tried to come up with a plan. "When he gets off the freeway, we smash out the window and make a break for it," Carter said.

"With what?" Nick asked. "It's not like you can break out a car window with your fist. And even if we could, where would we go? We're on foot and he has a car. Maybe we could attract the attention of another driver."

Carter shook his head. "What would we tell them? The doppelgänger looks just like your dad. And by now, they've probably copied all our parents. People would think we're wacko. They'd probably send us to a hospital or protective services."

Angelo pushed his glasses up on his nose. "We're running out of time. If our Evil Twins were telling the truth, we have less than a day to stop them. We can't afford to get caught up in some bureaucratic nightmare."

"Then what do we do?" Nick asked.

"Our best chance to escape is once we stop," Angelo said.

Carter took Carter Junior out of his shirt. The homunculus lay limp in his hands, his eyes halfway shut. "The first thing we have to do is get him back where he belongs. Look at the poor little guy. He's barely breathing."

Nick looked out the window and realized where they were headed. "He's taking us back to where we

found Carter Junior. Why would he do that?"

Angelo sighed. "I have no idea. But whatever it is, it can't be good."

For the rest of the ride, all they could do was sit and worry as the woods got closer and closer. When they turned off Highway 17 and pulled onto the fire road, Carter Junior sat up for a moment before collapsing back onto Carter's lap. Nick understood exactly how the homunculus felt. He'd been getting more and more tired as the trip went on until it was all he could do to keep his eyes open.

"How are you doing?" he asked Carter.

"Okay," Carter said, jaws cracking in a huge yawn. "I just need to take a little nap."

Evil Dad glanced into the rearview mirror and smiled.

"Don't go to sleep," Angelo said. "I think that's what they want."

At last they got off on the exit Nick's real dad had discovered on their camping trip. But instead of turning onto the gravel road that led to the campground, they continued straight on the fire road until they came to a small cabin.

Evil Dad got out of the car. Nick glanced at the woods beyond the cabin. This was their chance; they

222

couldn't be that far away from the campground. Angelo nodded and mouthed, *Get ready to run.*

But before any of them could make a move, the doppelgänger pulled open Nick's door and wrapped an arm around his neck. "Don't even think about trying to make a run for it," he said, squeezing until Nick could barely breathe. "You three do exactly what I tell you or you're going to be the two Monsterteers."

"Don't . . . listen to—" Nick gasped, before his father's doppelgänger squeezed so hard dots appeared in front of his eyes.

"Let go of him," Carter said. "We'll do what you say."

"Yes." Angelo nodded.

"Better," Evil Dad said, releasing his grip just enough that Nick could gulp a mouthful of air. "Now, into the cabin." He marched the tree boys up to the cabin door and pushed it open. "Get inside."

Nick squinted as Evil Dad shoved him through the door of the cabin. It was so dark inside he could barely see anything. As his eyes adjusted, he realized why. All the windows had been boarded over. He could just make out a small kitchen, a fireplace, and a table with a single chair in front of it.

Evil Dad herded them to a door on the other side of the table, unlocked the dead bolt, and motioned them

223

into the next room. "Look," Carter said. "It's the guy from the campsite."

Nick peered through the doorway. Mr. Grunwald, the German who had yelled at them before, was sitting on the floor with his head in his hands. He looked up wearily as Carter and Angelo entered the room.

A moment later, Evil Dad released his grip on Nick's neck and shoved him in the back, sending Nick stumbling into the room. Angelo caught him before he could fall and Nick spun around as his father's doppelgänger began to close the door. "You're just going to leave us here?" Nick asked. "We'll starve."

"You'll disappear long before that happens," the doppelgänger said. "Although you might get a little thirsty. Speaking of food, I have to get home in time for dinner. We're finally trying that new Italian place." He closed the door and Nick heard it lock behind him. A minute later he heard a car start and drive away.

Carter ran up to the door and slammed his body against it. He might as well have been throwing himself against a brick wall. The door was built of thick, solid redwood planks. Nick checked the only window in the room, but it was covered with the same thick boards. The only light came through a few spaces between the wood, barely wide enough to slip a finger through.

There was no way to get out.

Angelo turned toward Mr. Grunwald, who had put his head back in his hands. "Can you tell us what's going on?"

Nick thought the man would yell at them. Instead, he only shook his head and, without looking up, asked, "*Warum*? Why? Why didn't you tell me you take *Männchen*?"

"*Männchen*?" Nick asked.

The German pointed at the homunculus. "*Männchen*. Little man."

"It's my fault." Carter held out Carter Junior. "You can have him back."

The German shook his head sadly. "Is too late. He belong to you now."

"But he's sick." Carter wiped his eyes with one hand. "Can't you help him?"

"Not sick. Dying." The man rubbed his face with his hands. "Too long away from home and . . ." He sighed.

"We'll take him back," Carter said. "I know the spot where we found him."

Mr. Grunwald chuckled sadly. "*Ja.* Break down the walls and we all go free." He said a long string of words Nick didn't understand. But his meaning was very clear. They weren't going to escape the cabin anytime soon.

"Do you know about the doppelgängers?" Angelo asked.

The man nodded. "Ja."

"They've taken over our town," Nick said.

The man nodded again. "You have opened the *Türöffnung*. The doorway."

Nick dropped to the floor. He was so tired. "We're sorry. We didn't know."

"Isn't there some way to fix it?" Angelo asked. "I thought that if we brought the homunculus back it would make things right."

"*Ja*," the man said. "*Männchen* go back, return to Father Tree, door close, all fixed. *If* boys bring him back two days ago, one day ago, maybe. But now, too late."

"Father tree?" Angelo asked. He reached for his backpack before realizing it was no longer there, and Nick knew he'd been going for his monster notebook.

"Father Tree." The German nodded. "Father Tree source of doppelgänger and *Männchen*. Keeper of doorway." He held his hands up over his head and made a gesture like a huge creature walking through the woods. "Walks through woods. Watching. Protecting."

"Wait," Nick asked. "Does this Father Tree have really big feet?"

"*Ja*," Mr. Grunwald said. "Big feet."

226

"That's what made the footprints," Carter said.

"And probably what tried to warn us about the doppelgängers with the symbol," Angelo added. "I'll bet it came looking for the homunculus when it left to steal our cookies."

Nick tried to think. "So you're saying we opened some kind of doorway by taking Carter Junior out of the woods? But if we take him back to this Father Tree, we could close the door and bring the doppelgängers back?"

"*Sapperlot!*" the German said, slamming his bony hands against the cabin wall. "You can no get out. Even if you could, woods filled with doppelgängers now. Too dangerous."

"It can't be any more dangerous than what's going to happen to us here," Nick said.

Mr. Grunwald ran his fingers through his messy gray hair.

"What if we found a way to escape?" Carter asked. "What are our chances of making it to the Father Tree?"

Mr. Grunwald held his thumb and finger so close they were almost touching. "*Winzig.* Tiny."

Nick closed his eyes. "So what you're saying is there's no way to break out of this cabin. And even if there was, we'd never make it to the Father Tree

227

because the woods are full of doppelgängers now."

The German nodded. "*Ja.*"

"What about Carter Junior?" Carter asked. "If we stay out here, what happens to him?"

Mr. Grunwald shook his head.

"That's it then." Carter stood up. "I'm going for it."

Nick groaned. "Didn't you hear what he just told us?"

"It's my fault," Carter said. "I brought Carter Junior in and I'm taking him back."

"We're locked up tight," Angelo said. "And we don't even know where this Father Tree is."

"It's impossible," Nick agreed.

Carter smirked. "Impossible happens to be my specialty."

CHAPTER 24

AND THEY SAY YOU CAN'T LEARN ANYTHING FROM VIDEO GAMES

Carter stared around the small, dark room. "If I can only find something to cut through the boards."

"Sure," Nick said. "If you come across a chain saw, let me know."

Angelo walked over and examined the dead bolt on the door. It was the kind of lock that had a keyhole on both sides. "I don't imagine you have an extra key for this?"

Mr. Grunwald chuckled and pointed his thumb toward the boarded-over window. "*Ja. Ja.* In car. You escape, get key, and unlock door. Except you need key to escape."

Nick put his eye to one of the spaces between the

boards and peered out at an old green station wagon parked behind the cabin. The car was less than twenty feet away. And yet it might as well have been twenty miles for all the good it did them.

Carter edged up bedside Nick, peeking through another of the cracks. "The keys are in that car?"

"*Ja.*" The German nodded sadly. "In ignition."

"All right," Carter said. "So all we need to do is find a way to get the keys out of the car and we're good to go."

Nick patted him on the back. "Let me know when you figure out how to squeeze through a one-inch crack."

"Hang on a second," Angelo said. "There's one thing we've never figured out. How did the homunculus get into the car the night we went camping?"

Nick scratched his head. "Maybe it was unlocked."

"No." Angelo looked down at Carter Junior, who was resting in Carter's arms. "Your dad said he locked it, and you checked it. And even if he did get in through the door, how did the homunculus escape from the aquarium the night it disappeared?"

Carter patted Carter Junior's head. "He didn't escape. Stupid Kimber Tidwell took him."

Angelo shook his head. "I'm not saying she didn't. But let's say she opened the window and saw Carter Junior. Then what? She climbed in the window, took the books and the board off the aquarium, grabbed the homunculus, and put the books and board back on the aquarium, all without waking Carter up, when he was sleeping right there?"

Nick hadn't really thought about that before. It did seem strange that Kimber would put the board back in exactly the same spot before leaving. In fact, it didn't make sense at all. "So what are you suggesting?"

Angelo opened and closed his fingers as though squeezing his monster notebook. He turned to the German. "You said that the doppelgängers and the homunculus both come from the Father Tree?"

Mr. Grunwald nodded.

"The doppelgängers look like this freaky, faceless bark kind of thing when they aren't copying humans," Angelo said. "What does a homunculus look like in its natural form?"

The German rubbed his chin with his knobby fingers. "Could be branch. Could be fruit. All part of tree."

"A branch?" Nick asked, with a flash of understanding.

231

"That's it." Angelo beamed. "That's how the homunculus got into the car and out of the aquarium." He turned to Carter. "Your homunculus can squeeze through small spaces by turning into a branch."

"You're saying Kimber didn't take him?" Carter asked.

"Not at all." Angelo paced across the room. "She probably did sneak down to your house that night. And I'll bet she opened the window too. The homunculus must have seen her, escaped from the aquarium by turning into a branch, and went to the window, where she grabbed it. That would explain why she was keeping it inside a cage, *inside* a wooden chest. Because she'd seen what it could do and she didn't want it to escape." He pointed to the window. "You have to get Carter Junior to squeeze between the boards and take the keys from the car."

"I don't know," Carter said. "I don't think he's up to it."

"He has to be," Nick said. "It's our only chance of getting out of here. Our only chance of saving him."

Angelo grabbed a chair and kicked at one leg until it splintered off. Shoving the splintered wood between the boards, he jabbed at the window until it shattered.

232

Then he cleared away as much of the broken glass as he could.

Carter held the homunculus up so it could see through the window. "Can you do it?" he asked. "Can you get the keys?"

Carter Junior raised his head weakly. "Keys?"

"Yeah," Carter said. "Car keys. Like in *Need for Speed*. You know, *vrummmm, vrummmm*."

The homunculus perked up with interest at Carter's revving sound. "Keys." It looked through the window at the car. "*Vrummmm, vrummmm*." Slowly it lifted one hand to the small space between the boards. For a moment nothing happened. Then its hand and arm turned into a small leafy twig.

"That's it!" Carter cried. "He's doing it."

Once his arm was through the crack, Carter Junior changed his leg into a branch as well. He slid both his leg and arm as far as he could through the opening. His body turned into a gnarled, brown branch no thicker than a finger, and his head became a small, green fruit.

"Holy limeade," Carter muttered as the homunculus, now completely in plant form, wriggled and pushed its way through the opening until it emerged from the other side.

As soon as it was through the crack, the homunculus changed back into a little Carter Junior. "Keys, *vrummmm, vrummmm,*" it repeated, climbing over the windowsill and down the cabin wall. A moment later it appeared on the ground below.

Nick, Carter, Angelo, and Mr. Grunwald pressed their faces to the boarded window as the homunculus made its way across the uneven ground. It stopped by the door and looked up at the open car window.

"It doesn't have any way to get up," Nick said.

But the homunculus was more resourceful than he thought. Carter Junior searched the ground until he found a long, narrow branch, and carried it to the car, where he leaned it up against the door. Then, like a miniature tightrope walker, he scaled the branch. A foot or so below the open window, he flexed his knees, bent, and leaped through the window and into the car.

"Yes!" Carter, Nick, and Angelo shouted, pumping their fists in the air.

Even Mr. Grunwald raised his hands. *"Ja! Ja!"*

A few seconds later, the station wagon's engine roared to life.

"What's he doing?" Nick asked.

"Don't turn the keys!" Angelo yelled out the window. "Take them out of the ignition."

There was a loud *clunk,* and the station wagon jerked, then began rolling slowly forward.

"Oh, shoot," Carter whispered.

"What do you mean, *shoot?*" Nick said.

Angelo glanced nervously from the window to Carter. "What's it doing?"

Carter stepped away from the wall. "Remember when I told you guys I taught Carter Junior how to play *Need for Speed Most Wanted?*"

Nick nodded, a dull burn moving up his chest.

"Well, the thing is . . . I taught him how to use my steering wheel and pedal controllers. But he could only reach one at a time. Which meant that every time he tried to drive a car he always ended up—"

Suddenly the station wagon's engine revved and the car shot forward, dust and rocks pluming out from beneath its back tires.

"Look out!" Carter yelled. He, Nick, Angelo, and Mr. Grunwald dove for the other side of the room a moment before the front of the station wagon smashed through the wall of the cabin like a battering ram. Boards and logs splintered and flew through the air like toys. The car's headlights shattered and one of the front tires came all the way up into the room. Bits of wood, dust, and metal filled the air in a choking cloud.

235

As soon as the car stopped, Carter was on his feet. "Carter Junior!" he screamed. "Are you okay?"

"*Vrummmm, vrummmm,*" a weak voice said. There was a soft cough, and then nothing.

CHAPTER 25

I'M REALLY FALLING FOR THESE KIDS
THESE KIDS

Nick walked to where Carter was cradling Carter Junior in his arms. "Is he . . . ?"

"He's breathing," Carter said. "But just barely."

"You must get him to Father Tree," Mr. Grunwald said. "Now!"

"Can you drive us?" Angelo asked, eyeing the mashed-up front of the car.

"No time," the German said. "*Männchen* is going." He pointed into the woods behind the cabin. "Straight and down. Father Tree will be near *Türöffnung*. But be careful while doorway is open. Do not get sucked in or you will never come out. And do not take *Männchen* near doorway. *Türöffnung* will destroy him."

"Okay," Carter said, breaking into a trot.

Nick looked at Angelo. "You know trying to get through the woods is probably suicidal."

Angelo nodded. "If I'm going to die, I want to do it as a Monsterteer." Together they ran and caught up with Carter.

"So, uh, what's our plan?" Carter whispered as they entered the darkness of the woods.

"You mean other than getting destroyed by our Evil Twins?" Nick said, searching the shadowy forest around them.

Carter pushed so close against him their shoulders touched. "I was kind of hoping dying was Plan B. Or C. Or maybe even Z."

"One of you better come up with the plan," Angelo said. "I'm fresh out."

"All right." Carter stepped on a branch and all three boys jumped at the sound of the crack. "The first thing is don't step on any more sticks."

Nick wiped his sweat-covered hands on the front of his jeans. "You're not inspiring a lot of confidence in me. Does any of this look familiar to either of you? Which way should we go?"

Immediately Angelo and Carter pointed in opposite directions.

238

"I remember that rock," Angelo said, pointing to a half-buried boulder. Nick thought he might vaguely recognize it. But he wasn't sure.

"I never forget a cookie," Carter said. "And I'm telling you, the cookie trail went that way."

Two minutes in and they were already arguing. "Come on, guys," Nick said. "We have to work together here."

"All right," Angelo said. "Maybe it was a different rock. I have to admit, I'm not positive, and Carter does have a good memory for food."

"That's better," Nick said. "Now, what do we do if we see a doppelgänger?"

"Run," Carter said. "As fast as we can. And hope it's someone like Old Man Dashner. Did you see how he was jogging? If he went any slower he'd be going backward."

"Down," Angelo whispered. The three of them dropped to the ground. Angelo pointed into the trees thirty or forty feet ahead. "Something's coming."

Nick squinted into the darkness. He didn't see anything. Then he had it. A shadow was moving stealthily through the trees. He tried to make out what it was, but from this distance all he could make out was a figure a little shorter than him.

239

"Nick," a voice called out. "Angelo, Carter. Where are you guys?" The figure got closer.

Carter stood up. "Tiffany? What are you doing here?"

"Oh, thank goodness," Tiffany said, breaking into a grin. "Angie told me I'd find you guys up here. But I think I turned the wrong way and got lost."

"What are you doing here?" Nick asked.

"An excellent question." Tiffany adjusted her sunglasses. "I couldn't imagine what you guys would be doing at a remote location like this, but Angie was insistent that I come." She brushed a pine needle out of her hair and wrinkled her nose. "Did you meet that crazy man back by the road? He totally freaked me out. So what are you guys doing here anyway?"

Angelo narrowed his eyes. "Step into the sunlight."

Tiffany smiled uncertainly. "What?"

Nick looked from Angelo to Tiffany, understanding dawning on him. How could Angie possibly have told Tiffany where to find them? And even if she did, how would Tiffany get here? "Let me see your shadow," he said.

"Why are you acting this way?" Tiffany took a step

240

back, deeper into the shade of the trees. "I came here to help you."

Angelo picked up a thick branch off the ground. "Step into the light now."

Tiffany looked around, then shouted, "Here! They're over here!"

Nick broke into a run with Carter and Angelo right next to him. Tree branches slapped his face and arms, and it was hard to keep his footing on the uneven ground. Behind them, Tiffany continued to shout.

"Left," Angelo called as a man in a pair of blue coveralls appeared on their right. Nick recognized him as the guy who worked at the local gas station.

"Get back here, you kids!" the man yelled.

A few seconds later Angelo's mom appeared from behind a huge birch. Angelo began to slow, but Nick grabbed his arm. "Not real."

The next ten minutes were a blur of running and turning. Every time they thought they had escaped, another doppelgänger showed up. The woods seemed to be filled with them. Angelo fought them off with his branch when they got too close, but there were more coming and no time to stop.

Nick's legs ached and his lungs burned. "Can't . . .

go . . . . much . . . longer," he gasped.

Just then, three quick *pops* sounded like gunshots in the quiet of the woods. Nick turned to see their three Evil Twins standing less than twenty feet away. Without losing a beat, the three doppelgängers raced toward them.

Angelo pointed to a thick stand of saplings to the right. "That way."

Nick ran into the trees, covering his face against the stinging needles. Without any warning, the ground dropped out from under him. Whirling his arms, he tried to keep his balance, but he was going too fast and the drop was too steep.

"Look out!" Carter shouted, piling into him.

Angelo grabbed the two of them and might have stopped them from falling, but at that moment Evil Nick, Carter, and Angelo came flying through the trees as well, and suddenly all six of them were rolling, sliding, and flipping down a steep, rocky slope.

Nick's leg caught on a root and a sharp pain raced up his leg. Carter—or was it his Evil Twin?—slammed against a tree and cartwheeled down the slope. Either Angelo or his doppelgänger reached for Nick, but he missed his grip and flipped past like a rag doll. Slipping

and tumbling, Nick spotted Carter Junior rolling down the hill next to him. He reached out to grab the homunculus and at that moment, something slammed against Nick's head and everything went gray.

CHAPTER 26

LAST CHAPTER. HOLD ON TIGHT!

When he came to, Nick was lying in the crevice of a deep valley. Every part of his body ached, and for a minute everything was a blur. Rubbing his eyes, he recognized the gently burbling creek to his left. This was where they'd first found the homunculus.

"Give him to me," a voice said.

Nick turned to see Carter standing a few feet away. Nick tried to stand, but his right leg collapsed under him. "What are you talking about?" he asked.

"Carter Junior," Carter said. "Give him to me quick."

Nick looked down and realized he was holding the homunculus.

"It's h-him." Carter pointed to his left, and as Nick

looked in that direction all his pain disappeared, over-shadowed by terror.

The creature standing less than ten yards away was at least twelve feet tall, with a thick body and long arms. Its skin was rough and brown like tree bark, and its limbs were long and gnarled. Leaves and vines wrapped around it in a sort of cloak. But what Nick couldn't stop staring at was the creature's face—or at least where its face should have been.

There was a puckered knot hole that might once have been a mouth and a gaping black hole where a nose had been . . . what? Ripped off maybe? But above those was only blank, brown emptiness.

"It doesn't have any eyes," Nick whispered.

The creature must have heard him, because at that moment it lifted a dark glass orb in its twisted fingers. From inside the orb, a single golden eye glared balefully down at them. The eye swiveled between the three boys before fixating on Nick. The knot hole ripped open to reveal jagged black teeth.

"What are you doing here?" a deep voice rumbled. This was the Father Tree.

Carter looked toward it, his face white and his arms shaking. "We, um, brought back your, uh . . ."

The creature held out its orb and Carter stumbled

back a step. In Nick's hands, Carter Junior opened his eyes and tried to sit up. The eye in the orb swiveled toward them and the mouth opened again. The cracked black teeth were terrible. "Bring it to me."

Realizing he couldn't walk, Nick started to hand the homunculus to the Father Tree. But at that moment, another Carter stepped forward.

"Don't give it to him!" The second Carter pointed to the giant redwood they'd seen the first time they were here. It looked every bit as big as Nick remembered. But now, where the markings had been before, there was a doorway as black as night. Twigs and pine needles fluttered across the forest floor and disappeared into the doorway with a sound like an insect being zapped by a hot lightbulb.

The second Carter glared at the first Carter. "You're my Evil Twin. You're trying to send Carter Junior through the doorway."

"That's a lie," the first Carter said. He turned to Nick. "Quick, give him to me so we can give him to the Father Tree and close the door."

One of them was the real Carter and one of them was his doppelgänger. But which was which? Nick looked for their shadows, but the sunlight was blocked by the giant redwood, casting the whole valley in shadow.

"Don't you recognize me?" one of the Carters said.

The other Carter held out his hands. "Come on, dude, I'm your friend."

Angelo walked out of a small grove of trees, rubbing his head. "Which one of them is real?" Nick asked.

Angelo looked from one Carter to the other, before pointing to his right. "He is."

"No," said another Angelo, entering the grove from the other side. "*He* is."

Nick looked back and forth. Now there were two Carters and two Angelos.

"Quick," both the Carters said at once, "give him to me while we have our Evil Twins outnumbered."

Nick looked back and forth. It was like listening to a stereo recording of Carter's voice coming from the left and right, in the exact same tone and inflection.

One of the Angelos started forward, and the other one did too. "Don't go near my friends," the first Angelo said.

"Nice try," the second one said. "But they aren't going to fall for it."

Nick tried to get to his feet again, but his leg screamed in agony and he dropped back to the ground. Inside the redwood, the doorway began making a loud sucking noise like a vacuum caught on a piece of curtain. Nick

knew time was short, but what could he do?

The first Carter stepped forward. His eyes met Nick's. "You have to believe me."

In that moment he knew. Carter was right. They hadn't believed in him enough before. But now was the time to start. Nick handed the homunculus to the Carter he felt sure was real.

As soon as he had Carter Junior, the first Carter spun around, eyes wide with glee. "I've got it!" he screamed to the Angelos. "Throw the real Carter in the doorway!" Before Nick or Angelo could respond, Evil Angelo darted forward. He grabbed the second Carter and tugged him toward the opening in the tree.

"No!" Carter screamed, his eyes wide with terror. He tried to twist away, but Evil Angelo's grip was too strong. The real Angelo ran to help him as Nick tried to force his injured leg to hold his weight. But it was too late.

Carter grabbed the edge of the door, his mouth an O of horror. "No!" he screamed before being sucked inside with a sickening *zap!*

Nick's chest froze. What had he done? "Carter!" he shouted.

Evil Angelo laughed gleefully. "One down, two to go." He turned to Evil Carter. "Put that nasty little thing

into the doorway and let's get this over with."

Still holding the homunculus, the first Carter turned and handed Carter Junior back to Nick with a wink. "Sorry," he whispered, "I had to find out which Angelo was the doppelgänger." He turned to the real Angelo and shouted, "It's me, dude. Get him!"

Realizing he'd been tricked, Evil Angelo turned to run. But the real Angelo dove, knocking his double's legs out from under him. Together he and Carter dragged the doppelgänger to the *Türöffnung*.

"Stop," Evil Angelo cried, scratching and kicking. "We can make a deal. I'll copy someone else. I'll give you power. I'll do anything you want."

"What I want is for you to get lost," the real Angelo said. Together, he and Carter heaved the doppelgänger into the air and flung him into the doorway.

Evil Angelo let out a howl of rage just before he disappeared into the dark opening with a sound like an engine roaring to life.

Nick was so focused on the battle that he never noticed the person sneaking up behind him until a pair of hands grabbed Carter Junior and tried to rip him from Nick's grasp. Nick spun around to find his Evil Twin right next to him.

"Give him to me," Evil Nick growled.

"Never," Nick said, trying to keep his grip on the homunculus.

Angelo raced over, grabbing a big branch. Carter grabbed a rock the size of a softball.

"Get him," Evil Nick said. "He's trying to destroy Carter Junior."

"Which one's the real you?" Carter asked, looking left and right.

"I am," Nick said.

"I am," Evil Nick said at the same time.

Angelo raised his club, but it was clear he was just as confused as Carter.

"Come on, you idiots!" Evil Nick shouted. "Are you going to hit the doppelgänger or not?"

The doorway was now roaring so loudly it sounded like a chain saw running at full throttle.

"Hurry," the Father Tree said. "Time is growing short."

Nick looked at his friends. How could he possibly convince them he was the real Nick?

"What are you doing?" Evil Nick cried. "Can't you two ever do anything right?"

Listening to his Evil Twin, Nick realized that although the doppelgängers might have all their origi-nals looks, memories, and talents, there was one thing

he and his friends shared that the doppelgängers didn't have.

Trust.

He looked his two friends in the eyes, knowing they would always have his back. "I'm sure you guys will do the right thing."

Carter and Angelo glanced at each other and nodded. They glared at the doppelgänger. "Get him," they said together.

As soon as they had dragged Evil Nick into the *Türöffnung*, Angelo and Carter hurried over to Nick's side.

"Is he okay?" Carter asked, eyeing the homunculus.

Nick nodded and grinned. "I think he's actually asleep."

Carter laughed. "Another way he's just like me. He can sleep through anything." He reached down to take one of Nick's arms. "We'll help you take him back to the Father Tree."

"No." Nick shook his head. "You've earned that right." He handed the gently snoring homunculus to Carter.

Carter looked down at his miniature and sniffed. "I sure am a cute little guy."

251

Cradling the tiny figure to his chest like a baby, Carter walked toward the giant creature, which looked a little less terrifying now with its jagged teeth turned up in a smile. He held out the homunculus, legs trembling. "Sorry for taking him. I swear I'll never do it again."

The huge Father Tree stepped forward, its giant feet dragging in the dirt, and scooped up the homunculus. Wrapping the creature in its tree branch hands, it began to croon something that sounded like a mix of a lullaby and the wind blowing through the branches of a tall pine on a cool summer night.

Carter Junior opened his eyes and cooed. He looked at Carter, waved, and then began to climb up the bark of the gargantuan tree. As he climbed, he began to change from a miniature human into a creature of bark and leaves until, at last, he blended completely into the tree.

At the same time, a huge coughing sound came from the opening of the *Türöffnung*. Nick turned to see a dark, tornado-like cloud appear in the opening. The ghostly faces of all the doppelgängers from town swirled into it. A second later, the doorway snapped shut—once again, just a tree with strange markings.

As the Father Tree turned to shamble back into the

252

woods, Carter shouted, "See you, Carter Junior! Maybe I'll come back and visit you some time."

The Father Tree turned its orb eye down on Carter and growled from deep inside its dark maw.

Carter laughed nervously. "Um. Just kidding."

Angelo carefully helped Nick sit up. "Do you think you can walk?"

Nick looped an arm around Angelo's shoulder. "I'll give it a try."

Carter moved to his other side, helping him to his feet. The pain was bad, but Nick was pretty sure nothing was broken.

"Let's see if Mr. Grunwald has his car working," Angelo said. "We should probably try to get back today. I'm betting everyone is going to be awfully confused."

Nick rubbed the lump on his head. "I think I'm going to have a major headache tomorrow."

"Somehow," Angelo said, "I don't think you'll be the only one."

CHAPTER 27

JUST KIDDING—
THIS IS THE
LAST CHAPTER
LAST CHAPTER

Monday afternoon, Nick carefully got out of his seat when the final bell rang. Carter and Angelo helped him up. Fortunately his knee was just sprained. He'd explained his injuries away by claiming that he'd wiped out on his bike—an easy story to sell, since both his and Angelo's bikes had been pretty banged up by the time they got them back. Carter had to put his allowance for at least the next six months toward replacing his little sister's bike and his mother's mop.

"Check that out," Carter said, nodding toward Kimber Tidwell. She and her friends had stopped wearing hats and puffy skirts. They were now carrying around little dolls dressed in clothes that matched what they were wearing exactly. Apparently that was the next big trend. Nick thought it was a little freaky himself.

The funny thing was that although Torrie and Rebel still followed Kimber everywhere she went, their relationship seemed to have changed a little. The girls no longer accepted everything Kimber said. In fact, more than once, Nick had heard Kimber admit that maybe she was wrong and they were right. He wasn't sure how long it would last. But who knew?

In town, things were slowly getting back to normal. Apparently there had been several car accidents, plus multiple reports of break-ins, vandalism, and other oddities. Nick's father had awakened from an especially deep sleep to discover his car was gone. Fortunately, the police found it idling at a stoplight just off the freeway. The assumption was that whoever had stolen it had seen something that scared him off and had left the car on foot.

Interestingly enough, the Tidwells had not reported anything. Nick thought Kimber might have had something to do with that. She probably didn't want anyone asking what she'd been keeping inside a cage in her cedar chest.

Ms. Schoepf hadn't done any more musical

numbers, but she had been asking around about a substitute teacher who bore a vague resemblance to her
and had some very odd ideas about education. Old Man
Dashner hadn't changed at all. He was still as cranky
as ever.

"There's one thing I've been wondering," Carter
said as they stopped to wait for the light.

"What's that?" Nick asked, flexing his knee and gri-
macing.

"How did you know it was the real me in the woods?
It could have been my doppelgänger asking you to
believe in him."

Nick grinned. "I'd know you anywhere. It's the
Cheetos breath."

"Nice," Carter said. "Very nice."

"I've been wondering something too," Angelo said.
"You know how the doppelgängers said they were
really just the part of us that we keep hidden away?"

"Sure," Nick said. "Carter thinks we're both idiots.
My dad would rather go out to eat. And Ms. Schoepf
has secret dreams of being a rock star."

Angelo put a hand over his mouth. "That means that
when Angie told you that you were handsome and—"

Nick slugged Angelo hard enough that his friend
winced in pain.

Carter howled with laughter. "Nick and Angie, sitting in a tree. K-I-S-S-I-N-G."

When the boys got to Nick's house, they found Nick's dad in the kitchen. Nick limped over and patted his dad on the shoulder. "What's that for?" Dad said, looking up.

"I just wanted to tell you that it doesn't matter where we go, or what you might forget—you're the best dad ever. And I love going on vacations with you, no matter how crazy they are."

Dad smiled a sly little grin. "Funny you should say that." He called up the stairs. "Honey, come here quick. I have something to tell you."

Mom came down the stairs with pieces of foil wrapped around her hair. "What's wrong? I was tinting my hair."

"It's not what's wrong," Dad said, beaming from ear to ear. "It's what's right. I just got an email from the company that messed up our reservation."

Mom moaned. "You called me out to talk about the camping trip again?"

"Not the camping trip," Dad said. "Something much, much bigger. It seems the computer glitch was big enough that hundreds of people's vacations were ruined. So to avoid a class-action lawsuit, they offered

everyone their choice of ten different vacations. All expenses paid."

Mom's eyes lit up. "Please tell me it's a cruise. I've always wanted to go on one."

"Even better," Dad said. "Listen to this. During winter break, while everyone else is cold and wet, all five of us are going to take part in an archeological exploration of a newly discovered pyramid, smack-dab in the middle of a Mexican rain forest. And the kicker is . . . it's cursed!"

Looking Back

And so, our friends live to fight another day. And fight they will. For, like you, they cannot sit back and wait for adventure to come to them. They seek it out, drink it like cool, life-giving water. They thrive on it.

No doubt, they will soon come across something else not of the world most people see. And when they do, I will be here documenting it for your reading pleasure. Because you too will be back. You're just that kind of person.

And speaking of seeing, I've been staring into the looking glass more and more lately, and a disturbing thought has occurred to me. What if the face I see there is not my reflection at all, but I am a reflection of it? What if I am the dark doppelgänger trapped in a world I cannot escape?

Try not to think about that next time you see yourself in the mirror.

Sincerely,

B. B.

ACKNOWLEDGMENTS

Normally, I would thank all the people who have helped me make my book—my agent, my editor, my family, the amazing artist who does the cover.

Except last week something weird happened. They all disappeared. It's like they went on a big vacation without me. In their places are these evil twin "humans" who *look* like them but act almost exactly the opposite.

Mike "Shotgun" Bourret, who shoots down all my best ideas; Andy "Rhyming" Harwell, who thinks I should write all my books in verse; a bunch of mean people that write all over my pages in red ink, Ann "You missed a comma" Lyon, Heath "That's so lame" Moore, Lu "This is a plot?" Staheli, Shelly "That was romance?" Holmes, Rah "My kid could write better" Eden, and Robby "You get an F" Wells; Douglas "Stick figure" Holgate, who clips out magazine pictures and calls them a cover; Sarry "You've got page numbers be happy" Kaufman, who barely gave me page numbers; Rose "You're lucky to get a book" Brosnan, who told me to stop complaining and write something else; a bunch of hooligans by the names of Killer E, Big Nick, Scott "Two Face," Naughty Nat, Jake the Snake, and Nick the Blade, who took my advance and spent it all on candy; and Jenny "Gray Bar" Savage, who claims to be my wife but keeps me locked in the basement slaving away on more stories to earn bread and water.

And these ingrates: Jamie "Maze Runner" Dashner, Kim "Too Cool" Tidwell, Syd "The Enforcer" Schoepf, and Rebel "Just Rebel" Benson, who are all demanding payment for using their names.

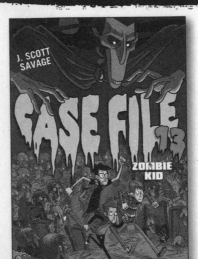

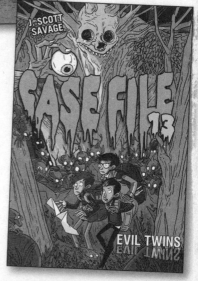